"Mind If I Join You?" Deacon Prescott To Her On The Arcade Love Seat Without Waiting For An Answer.

"I guess not," Kylie said wryly.

"I knew you wouldn't."

"Really? Why is that?" she asked.

"Because of fate," Deacon said.

"Fate?" To Kylie, the man who'd boldly taken the seat beside her didn't look like he left much to destiny. There was a will of pure steel under his five-hundred-dollar suit.

"Angel, I'm all about chance and luck," he answered.

She couldn't help but smile. Deacon Prescott was very charming, but his manner had an air of ritual to it. She might be unsophisticated, but she had the feeling she wasn't the first woman to hear these lines from him. Knowing this, Kylie tried her best not to be interested in him, but she knew she was holding a losing hand....

Dear Reader,

Welcome to another compelling month of powerful, passionate and provocative love stories from Silhouette Desire. You asked for it…you got it…more Dynasties! Our newest continuity, DYNASTIES: THE DANFORTHS, launches this month with Barbara McCauley's *The Cinderella Scandal.* Set in Savannah, Georgia, and filled with plenty of family drama and sensuality, this new twelve-book series will thrill you for the entire year.

There is one sexy air force pilot to be found between the pages of the incomparable Merline Lovelace's *Full Throttle,* part of her TO PROTECT AND DEFEND series. And the fabulous Justine Davis is back in Silhouette Desire with *Midnight Seduction,* a fiery tale in her REDSTONE, INCORPORATED series.

If it's a whirlwind Vegas wedding you're looking for (and who isn't?) then be sure to pick up the third title in Katherine Garbera's KING OF HEARTS miniseries, *Let It Ride.* The fabulous TEXAS CATTLEMAN'S CLUB: THE STOLEN BABY series continues this month with Kathie DeNosky's tale of unforgettable passion, *Remembering One Wild Night.* And finally, welcome new author Amy Jo Cousins to the Desire lineup with her superhot contribution, *At Your Service.*

I hope all of the Silhouette Desire titles this month will fulfill your every fantasy.

Melissa Jeglinski

Melissa Jeglinski
Senior Editor, Silhouette Desire

Please address questions and book requests to:
Silhouette Reader Service
U.S.: 3010 Walden Ave., P.O. Box 1325, Buffalo, NY 14269
Canadian: P.O. Box 609, Fort Erie, Ont. L2A 5X3

Let
It
Ride
KATHERINE
GARBERA

Published by Silhouette Books
America's Publisher of Contemporary Romance

SILHOUETTE BOOKS

ISBN 0-373-76558-4

LET IT RIDE

Copyright © 2004 by Katherine Garbera

Visit Silhouette at www.eHarlequin.com

Printed in U.S.A.

Books by Katherine Garbera

Silhouette Desire

The Bachelor Next Door #1104
Miranda's Outlaw #1169
Her Baby's Father #1289
Overnight Cinderella #1348
Baby at His Door #1367
Some Kind of Incredible #1395
The Tycoon's Temptation #1414
The Tycoon's Lady #1464
Cinderella's Convenient Husband #1466
Tycoon for Auction #1504
Cinderella's Millionaire #1520
In Bed with Beauty #1535
Cinderella's Christmas Affair #1546
Let It Ride #1558

*King of Hearts

KATHERINE GARBERA

has had fun working as a production page, lifeguard, secretary and VIP tour guide, but those occupations pale when compared to creating worlds where true love conquers all and wounded hearts are healed. Writing romance novels is the perfect job for her. She's always had a vivid imagination and believes strongly in happily-ever-after. She's married to the man she met in Walt Disney World's Fantasyland. They live in Central Florida with their two children. Readers can visit her on the Web at katherinegarbera.com.

To my parents, David and Charlotte Smith,
who never say no when it's in their power to say yes,
and who always support me with their love.

ACKNOWLEDGMENTS:

Thanks to Mary Louise Wells
who took time out of her busy schedule to help me.
Thanks also to Allie Pleiter who was my partner in
adventure in Vegas. I think we're the only two people
to visit Sin City and not gamble a cent!
Also thanks to Blossom and Bubbles—
it'd be no fun fighting crime
(or writing romance) without you two!—Buttercup

Prologue

"**D**id you discover anything being a woman?" Didi asked me when I appeared in front of her.

The body-disappearing thing still made me crazy. Twenty-five years as a mob *capo* ordering hits and living large had not prepared me for life after death. I'd cut a deal with God, or rather with Didi, God's emissary at the Pearly Gates. And now I was a freakin' matchmaker to the lovelorn. It wasn't as bad as I made out to Didi, but the skinny-angel broad got on my nerves and I didn't want her to know that I actually liked doing these good deeds.

However, I didn't like the surprise she'd left me with last time, sending me to Earth in a woman's body. No man should ever have that experience. "I didn't," I answered her. "This time I want an assignment where I get to be a guy. Not an old fart, either."

"Was it a hard adjustment?" she asked. I didn't like her tone. But then, I didn't have to like her. Staying up here, instead of going to hell, was a heck of a deal.

"Let's skip to the good part. Just give me one where I can be a guy."

A large pile of file folders materialized on the desk. I took pride in the fact that though the stack still was big, it was lighter by two.

She smiled at me, which I didn't trust. Despite being an angel, this one had a mean streak in her.

"How about one in Vegas?" she asked.

Now I really didn't trust her when she was being nice to me. "Am I going to be a showgirl?"

She laughed. She wasn't half-bad-looking when she smiled. "Not this time."

She was trying to scare me again. It wasn't going to work. I'd faced a man with a loaded Glock and hadn't quivered.

"This one is special."

Special. The word echoed in my head and I shuddered. *Merda,* I didn't know if getting to heaven was worth all of this. "How special?"

"You'll see," was all she said.

I opened the file and scanned it. The chick, Kylie

Smith, was a secretary from Los Angeles. The guy, Deacon Prescott—he was my kind of guy. He'd grown up on the streets and worked as an enforcer for the Vegas mob.

"This one doesn't look so tough," I said to Didi.

"Good. Then you won't have any problems."

My body dissolved before I could retaliate. Didi liked having the last word. But that was okay. I was on the Vegas strip, standing in front of one of the newer casinos, and for the first time since I'd died, I felt like my fate wasn't so bad.

One

Deacon Prescott leaned closer to the ten-inch security monitor and found the woman of his dreams. Her features were indistinguishable. But every other detail was perfect.

Her brown hair was caught at the back of her neck; her clothing was understated—elegant. He zoomed the camera in for a closer look.

"Perfect," he muttered. She was everything he'd been searching for. She had classic bone structure and a sedate hairstyle, everything he'd been hoping to find in a wife and never expected to see in the lobby of his hotel/casino, the Golden Dream.

She surveyed the lobby. Damn. She was probably

here with a boyfriend or husband. He adjusted the camera's zoom lens—she wasn't wearing a wedding ring. Her green eyes were wide-set and her features delicate. She was an ordinary woman in the real world, but out of place in the garish world that was his life.

At thirty-eight it was well past time for him to settle down and start a family. And the only thing that had been holding him up was the right woman. A woman who could be that other half of his life without engaging his emotions. If he'd learned anything from a lifetime in Vegas, it was that fortune changed on the roll of the dice. Happiness in life and forever love were only illusions.

"What are you staring at?"

Deacon glanced over his shoulder at Hayden MacKenzie—Mac to his friends. Mac owned the Chimera Casino and Resort. The Chimera was the second-most successful operation in Vegas behind the Golden Dream.

Mac was one of the few people Deacon called friend. Mac knew Deacon from his days of running in the gray area that bordered on lawlessness, and he'd used his influence to show Deacon another way to make a living. Deacon. He freely admitted that he'd learned most of what he knew about moving in the moneyed class from Mac.

"Nothing," Deacon replied.

Mac leaned over his shoulder at the enlarged picture of the woman. Her face filled the screen. Mac snickered. "Oh, is that what we're calling women these days?"

"Let me see her," Angelo Mandetti said. Mandetti was from the gaming commission. He was observing Deacon's operation as part of an annual review process. The man had been in his hotel for a week already, and Deacon respected him. He reminded him of one of the guys who used to hang around his mom when he was little. A guy who'd noticed Lorraine Prescott's skinny kid and taken time for him.

Mac stepped back and Mandetti leaned over the monitor. He let a low wolf whistle escape.

"She's not just a woman," Deacon said.

"What is she, then?" Mac asked.

"Nothing…yet," Deacon said. Mac had something Deacon had always wanted. The easy confidence that came from being raised with every privilege. Though they were the same age, Deacon often felt much older. Deacon wanted assuredness, and the woman in the security camera was the key to the life he'd always wanted.

"Meaning?" Mac asked.

"She's going to be my wife."

"Your wife?" Mandetti asked. "Congratulations, man."

Mac snorted. "He's never met her."

"Really?" Mandetti leaned closer to the screen,

observing the woman again. "She doesn't look like your type."

Deacon shrugged. He didn't say it out loud, but that was precisely why he wanted her.

Deacon watched as the woman took a book from her handbag and started reading. He had a glimmer of doubt. What if she was too staid to tame the restlessness inside him? Honorable men didn't cheat on their wives. He'd have to see if there was a spark of attraction between them before he settled on her as his wife.

"I'll be right back."

"This should be interesting."

Mac and Mandetti both moved to follow him. "Stay here."

Mandetti held his hands up and moved back from the door. Mac chuckled and sank into one of the leather chairs in the security booth. "It's not like we can't watch from here."

Deacon left the state-of-the-art room without comment. Walking down the long quiet hallway that housed the office of the front-desk manager and the casino-floor supervisor, he tried to plan what he would say to her.

He straightened his designer tie and opened the door that led to another world. The world that he'd lived in since he'd been old enough to walk. A world of ostentatious lights, ringing bells and spinning roulette wheels. He paused for a moment to look at his kingdom.

Pride in what he'd accomplished filled him, and he knew, if the woman showed the least bit of promise in the realm of sexual compatibility, he'd seduce her into becoming Mrs. Deacon Prescott. The queen of his little kingdom.

His journey through the casino was anything but quick. He was stopped by regulars and by a recently hired dealer who wanted to talk about a new invention he had for dealing. Deacon rang his secretary, Martha, and had her schedule the dealer for an appointment at the end of his shift. Finally he was out of the casino and in the lobby. He glanced around for the woman.

Suddenly all the suave lines he'd cultivated over the years left him, and he couldn't think of a thing to say. He was back on the streets for a moment, the grubby little boy looking at the glamour he could never touch.

He smoothed his hands down the sides of his pants and stood a little taller. He was Deacon Prescott, dammit. *Entrepreneur* magazine's Man of the Year two years running. Certainly no *ordinary* woman could keep him from achieving his goal.

Kylie Smith heard someone approach. The Golden Dream was a classy hotel with Old World charm, but the men who frequented the casino weren't as classy. She'd been approached by four different guys while waiting for her friend.

Unwanted male attention made her uncomfortable. And she knew it wasn't because she was drop-dead gorgeous. It was only because she seemed available.

She'd pulled back her hair into a haphazard ponytail, put on her reading glasses, complete with "grandma" chain, to keep from losing them, and she held her favorite classic novel. Her outfit should have been daunting enough to deter even the most determined male. But this person didn't go away. Maybe it was Tina. One glance over the edge of her book and she realized it wasn't. Unless Tina had taken to wearing Italian men's loafers, which seemed highly doubtful. She turned away from the man and tried to concentrate on *The Scarlet Pimpernel.*

Except the man smelled good. He had on some kind of cologne with a woodsy scent that made her want to take a deeper breath. She glanced up quickly, from her book, with the intent of averting her gaze quickly but he stopped her.

His features weren't classically handsome but there was something arresting in those gray eyes. Something that hinted at hidden passion and inner fire—two things she'd never had. Nervously Kylie pushed her glasses farther up her nose and tried to put on a calm face.

Attractive men simply didn't talk to her.

"Hello," he said. His voice was deep, not a soft sophisticated sound but a gravelly one that awakened senses she'd thought had gone into a coma.

"Hi," she said. Yes, she was the queen of scintillating conversation.

"Mind if I join you?" he asked. He sat down next to her on the brocade love seat without waiting for an answer.

"I guess not," she said wryly.

"I knew you wouldn't."

"Really? Why is that?"

"Because of fate."

"Fate?" This guy didn't look as if he left much to destiny. She sensed a will of pure steel under that thousand-dollar suit.

"Angel, I'm all about chance and luck."

"Those are decidedly different from fate." In response to his raised eyebrows, she stumbled on. "Fate implies that something is destined. Luck—not so much."

"Depends on whether or not you're fated to have good luck."

She couldn't help with smile. He was very charming, though his charm had an air of ritual to it. She had the feeling she wasn't the first woman to hear those lines.

"How about dinner?" he asked.

"I don't know you," she said.

He stood. "Deacon Prescott."

She took the hand he held out and tried to shake it, but he grasped only her fingers. With his thumb he caressed her knuckles, then brought her hand to his lips and pressed a warm kiss to the back of it.

She shivered. More than the hotel had Old World charm.

"And you would be?"

"Kylie Smith."

"May I join you, Kylie?"

She wanted to pretend not to be interested, but she was. Before she could answer, he sat down again this time, leaving only six inches of space between them. Kylie felt crowded. He was long and lean, but there was a breadth to his shoulders that made her feel small, delicate even.

"What are you doing here?" he asked.

"I'm waiting for someone."

"A man?"

"That's none of your business."

"Fair enough. What brings you to Vegas?" he asked, sliding his arm along the back of the love seat. His heat and scent surrounded her. Tempted to lean into his touch, she scooted farther away, instead.

"Girls' weekend out."

He gave her a half smile and tucked a strand of hair behind her ear. She shivered with awareness. She simply wasn't a touchy person by nature. And it'd had been a long time since anyone had touched her, unless you counted her mom, who always hugged her when they met weekly for brunch.

"You have beautiful hair," he said.

Was he hitting on her? Kylie could never be sure if a man was just being friendly or really interested in her. She wished for a minute she was more like Tina, who flitted from one man to the next, enjoying what each had to offer.

But she never had been. She'd been raised to believe that settling down and raising a family was a good thing. And it was something she'd always wanted.

Even after her failed marriage, she still wanted to find the right guy and have kids. But that didn't mean she wanted to meet him in Vegas. She scooted still farther away and tottered for a moment on the edge of the seat. He grabbed her arm and pulled her back.

"Why are *you* in Vegas, Deacon?"

"I live here," he said as if nothing had happened.

"Do you really? Sorry, don't answer that. All the bells have rattled my brain."

He laughed and it was a kind sound, seeming almost strange coming from a man who looked as dark and forbidding as he did. Jet-black hair and tanned olive complexion. He had large hands. On his pinky was a rough-looking gold ring with some sort of insignia she didn't recognize.

Realizing she'd been staring at him too long, she glanced up to see if he'd noticed. He had. He touched her face with one finger. Why was he touching her? She should pull away.

But she couldn't. An indefinable emotion in his eyes froze her in place. The intensity of his gaze on her made her feel special. Made her feel as if she was a fairy-tale princess and he was a knight willing to slay dragons for her. Made her feel for once as if she wasn't staid and safe, but the kind of woman a man would choose for a vacation fling.

But she wasn't really any of those things. Her stomach growled and Kylie blushed.

"My offer for dinner still stands," he said.

"I'm reading a really good book," Kylie said. That had to be the lamest excuse she'd ever come up with.

"The day a book holds more excitement for a woman than I do is a sad one."

"Prepare to cry." She wanted to say yes. In fact, she thought, closing the book and putting it in her purse, she was going to. But she didn't want it to be that easy for him.

"Come on. It'll be fun," he cajoled.

"Fun? I'm not sure I'm ready for fun."

"How about friendly?"

She'd come to Vegas to live a little, and sitting in her room reading didn't sound exactly exciting. There was something in Deacon's eyes that promised more than fun and friendly, and Kylie was sick of always being...herself.

"Sure. I'd love to."

"Meet me back here in an hour."

"An hour?"

"Fate takes time."

"Then it's not really fate."

He shrugged.

"What should I be prepared for?" she asked.

"To be swept off your feet," he said with a wink and walked away.

Two

Deacon returned to the security booth after calling his secretary to find out where Kylie was staying. He was pleased when he discovered she was a guest at his hotel. He'd made arrangements for a picnic dinner to be prepared by the Golden Dreams head chef. He also called the bellman and ordered his Jaguar to be brought around front. Then he called the flower shop and had a bouquet sent to Kylie's room.

"Smooth work down there," Mandetti said when Deacon reentered the security room.

"Yeah, I especially liked the part where she almost fell off the bench trying to get away from you," Mac said with a grin.

Deacon ignored them, his mind on Kylie. She had returned to her room. Thanks to Martha, he knew she was in the east tower, room 1812. He keyed up her hallway on the monitor. It was empty. He tried not to think about her as a woman. She was the means to an end. The faceless model in the Ralph Lauren ad wearing a cable-knit sweater and holding a child.

Except she wasn't a faceless woman. She was Kylie Smith, a woman with sharp wit and a sense of humor. He hadn't expected humor from her. He'd never really considered that as a qualification for the right family.

Mac leaned over his shoulder again. "You got it bad."

"Got what?" Deacon asked.

"The lust bug."

"Ha. This has nothing to do with lust." That wasn't entirely true, but Deacon didn't discuss women with Mac, because they tended to disagree about them on a fundamental level. Deacon had been raised by his mom and surrounded by show-girls. Mac had been raised by his father, a bitter man who hated all women. Mac's attitude toward women was that they were after only one thing—money. Deacon had seen firsthand how money could make the difference between life and death to a woman on the streets.

"She doesn't seem like the one-night-stand type," Mandetti said.

Deacon knew that; his intentions toward her were noble. Kylie was even better-suited to the label in his head that read *WIFE* than he'd thought she'd be.

"I can't believe you, old man," Mac said.

"What's not to believe?" He turned to Mandetti. "Doesn't she look like marriage material?"

Mandetti nodded.

Mac leaned against the wall, crossing his arms over his chest. "You really think you're going to marry her."

Deacon shrugged. Unless he'd lost his touch, hell, yeah, he was going to marry Kylie.

"She won't do it," Mac said.

"She might," Mandetti said.

Mac could be right. But when he put his mind to something, Deacon never lost. He'd carved a life for himself many wanted but few ever achieved. He wasn't one of those guys who accepted defeat. Nothing gave Deacon the thrill wagering did. Though Kylie had the potential, he thought. "Wanna bet?"

"Now you're talking," Mac said. "Terms?"

"There are no terms. If I convince her to marry me, I win." Deacon liked things simple.

"Okay, but you do it in two weeks. And it has to be a real marriage."

Two weeks, was that enough time? Kylie was a little skittish, but he'd handle her carefully.

"Deal. When I win, you can finance a new addition to the children's shelter," Deacon said. One of the first things he'd done when he'd made his fortune was to finance a children's shelter for Vegas kids. A place to keep them off the streets while their parents gambled or worked in casinos.

"Okay. When I win, you can finance a medieval-sword display at the Chimera." Mac's hotel/casino was known for its world-renowned traveling displays.

Mandetti's cell phone rang, and he turned to take the call. Deacon heard him curse in Italian. "Give me a break, angel. I'm just getting started here."

"See? Women are nothing but trouble," Mac said. Mandetti covered the mouthpiece. "I better take this outside. I'm going to be observing your operation on the floor tonight, right?"

"Yes. I'll join you after midnight. I'll have Peter meet you in the lobby in fifteen minutes, okay?"

Mandetti nodded and left the room. Mac followed him out.

Deacon settled back in one of the empty chairs in the security room. A small team of three men were always on shift. A glass wall separated them from Deacon and his bank of monitors. He'd had the room designed so he could come in and observe whenever he wanted without disturbing the security operation. Also, it allowed him to train new hires without disrupting the workflow.

Kylie emerged from her room, and he watched her pause in the hallway. She chewed her lower lip and turned back to her door. She was going to stand him up, he thought.

She went into her room. Deacon reached for his cell phone, dialed the front desk and asked to be connected to her room. Kylie needed some coaxing.

She answered on the second ring. Her voice had a sexy breathless quality.

"Hey, angel," he said, trying for a lightness he didn't feel. It shouldn't matter to him if she changed her mind. If he lost the bet with Mac, he'd be out a bit of money but hardly enough to break him. And it wasn't as if there weren't other respectable women in the world. But there was something about Kylie Smith he wanted.

"Deacon?"

"Who else?"

"I don't think you know me well enough to call me angel," she said. The tart note in her voice would have done a schoolteacher proud.

"I will after tonight," he said. The sensual promise he'd seen in her eyes earlier guaranteed it.

He remembered that scared moment when she'd almost bolted, but then found her sass and stayed. He knew she wanted to have dinner with him. But he also knew that her life to date had conditioned her and he was moving too fast. He'd have to find a way around her objections.

"Um…about that…"

"Not going to back out now, are you?" Deliberately he pitched his voice low. He'd been told by one of his ex-girlfriends that she'd do anything for him when he asked her in that tone.

"Well…"

She was wavering. "Take a chance. This is Vegas, angel, and you're not living it unless you take a risk."

"Are you risky?" she asked.

"Not for you," he said, surprised to realize he meant it. He wanted her to feel safe with him. Safe and secure. And sure that he wasn't going to wine her, dine her and then walk away in the morning.

"It's just dinner," he said after a few moments of silence.

She hesitated. He heard the catch in her breath. She was going to say no.

"Okay. I'll be down in a few minutes," she said.

"Good."

He disconnected and headed for the lobby. Again his trip through the casino was slow. He entered the lobby and paused. Kylie was waiting for him by the fountain. But she hardly resembled the woman he'd originally seen in the security camera.

Her hair fell in soft waves to her shoulders, her sundress delineated the curves of her body, and her long legs were bare. A wave of lust hit him hard.

And he knew himself well enough to know that waiting for her, seducing her slowly, was going to be hell.

Kylie had changed her mind and her clothes about fifty times in the hour since she'd left the lobby and Deacon Prescott. If it wasn't for Deacon's phone call, she'd be sitting in her room, eating a room-service cheeseburger and reading *The Scarlet Pimpernel.* But instead, she was in the lobby waiting for a man who made her heart beat double time and who had awakened her senses with his touch.

That didn't gibe with the sensible administrative assistant she was in her normal life. She'd thought about having a reality check. Calling her mom and listening to all the reasons that sane, sensible Kylie shouldn't be in Vegas. But she was tired of being sane and sensible.

She'd checked in with her girlfriends before leaving for the evening. And they were prowling the casinos tonight with some guys they'd met earlier. They'd all made plans to meet in the lobby bar just after midnight.

She glanced at her watch and then around the lobby. Her breath caught in her throat. Deacon walked toward her with the self-assured stride of a successful man. His suit jacket was buttoned and his silk tie perfectly knotted. He stopped to exchange pleasantries with a few people on his way to her.

Their eyes met and held for a moment. It seemed

as if only she and Deacon existed in the lobby. His gaze skimmed down her body, stirring all her senses to life and making her blood flow heavier.

He moved very close to her. His scent surrounded her and she breathed it in deeply. She wished she was more like Deacon just then, who could reach out and touch someone he was attracted to whenever he wanted. Her fingers tingled with the need to touch him.

"You look lovely," he said, sliding an arm around her shoulders and brushing her cheek with a kiss.

His words threw her because she was the "nice" sister. Not the pretty one. Not the smart one. *Just the nice ordinary one.* She knew she wasn't any man's definition of lovely. Even with his intense gray eyes shining with sincerity.

She stepped back, not knowing how to take him. No man had ever made her feel what he did. A million and one different things at once. And she wanted to believe. Believe that this was the one man who'd see her and she'd be lovely in his eyes, but she doubted it.

"That was a compliment," he said, slipping his hand under her elbow and leading her out of the hotel. "You're supposed to say thank-you."

"Sorry to disappoint you," she said.

"You didn't. But there was something in your eyes that said you may not believe me."

"That's because my dad's Irish and I heard my share of blarney growing up."

"I can't be the first man to compliment you."

She tugged her arm from his grip and pulled her purse strap higher on her shoulder. She didn't want to have this conversation.

"Can we talk about something else?" she asked. She was tempted to believe him. The way she'd believed Jeff's lies. But she wasn't an eighteen-year-old girl anymore, and the woman she was at twenty-eight was a lot smarter. Yeah, right, she thought.

He deliberately took her arm again and continued leading her through the lobby. They reached the bell stand and the valet led them to a Jaguar convertible out front. "Your car, Mr. Prescott."

"Thank you, Scott," Deacon said, slipping the man a folded bill.

"Mr. Prescott, a moment?" said another man from the hotel entrance.

"Do you mind, Kylie?"

"Not at all," she said.

Kylie suspected that Deacon was more than a guest at the Golden Dream casino. He held the door for her and she slid into the leather passenger seat, then watched while Deacon went to talk to the man. He returned in less than five minutes. And they headed away from the lights of the Vegas strip and out of the city.

The radio was tuned to a jazz station playing Ella

Fitzgerald singing "Blue Skies." The sun was setting in the west and her hair was blowing around her shoulders. She closed her eyes and tipped her head back. The warm wind caressed her skin, and for once she didn't think about being the nice ordinary sister.

"You're not just a guest at the casino, right?" she asked.

"I own the Golden Dream," he said.

She tilted her head and glanced at him. He wore a pair of aviator-style sunglasses and he held the wheel easily in his strong hands. His profile was chiseled and raw. There was something very masculine about him that called to everything feminine in her. The tension and pressure she'd felt while waiting for him in the lobby was slowly unwinding.

At this moment in the car with him, with the sun setting and the wind in her hair, she knew she belonged here. She'd never had such a sense anywhere before but in the small garden of her equally small house.

"How does one train to own a casino? Is there a casino school?" she asked.

"There might be. I learned the ropes working at other places on the strip."

"You must have been employee of the month," she said.

"Not quite," he said with a wry grin.

A few more miles passed and she realized they'd

left Vegas well behind and there didn't appear to be any restaurants on the highway unless you counted the small barbecue joint on the side of the road. But he didn't slow as they approached it.

"Where are we going to dinner?" she asked.

"Somewhere private."

"Oh," she said. Excitement tingled in her veins and she laced her fingers together to keep from nervously tucking her hair behind her ear.

"Don't sound so scared. I'm not the big bad wolf."

But when he smiled at her with all those teeth in that sexy face, she wished that he was the big bad wolf and that she was on the menu.

Deacon pulled off the highway and followed a road that led to a deserted stretch of land. He brought the car to a stop. The sun had set and the moon was rising over the horizon. When he was younger, the desert had always been a place to get away from the pressures of life in the city and to hide out. He still left the strip behind for the quiet nothingness of the land when things got too crazy.

Tonight his motives were simple. He wanted a chance to get to know Kylie without the pressure of knowing that any public place they went they'd be on camera. And knowing Mac as well as Deacon did, he knew he'd get some sort of critique of his behavior with Kylie.

"Is this the spot?" she asked, nervously finger-combing her hair.

It fell in soft waves around her shoulders. The wind from riding in the convertible had added to the fullness of the long dark curls. He reached out and touched one of them, then wrapped a smooth strand around his finger. God, she was worlds too soft for him.

He had no business taking this sweet young woman to the desert. Out here he always felt as if he could strip away the sophisticated layer he had to add in Vegas. Once he shed that layer, there was nothing left but the tough guy who was raised on the streets and conned his way up to the top.

This woman, with her innocent questions about casino school, had revealed more than she'd ever know with that one query.

"Deacon?"

"Yes."

"Are we getting out here? Are we going to have a picnic?" she asked. A hint of nervousness permeated her words.

"Yes to both."

"Can I help?"

"No. Tonight is just for you," he said as he climbed out of the car. "Why don't you flip through the CDs and find one you like, while I take care of everything."

He removed the cashmere blanket from the trunk

and quickly set up their picnic dinner. He opened the bottle of wine to let it breathe and then put out the china plates.

The dinner the chef had provided was still warm from the bags it had been packed in. He heard the throaty sounds of Louis Armstrong come from the car and then Kylie appeared at his side.

He got her seated on the blanket and served her dinner. She sat nervously next to him picking at her food. "Relax," he said at last.

"I'm trying. This just isn't my scene," she said, gesturing to the picnic items.

"Not the outdoorsy type?" he asked. Truth be told, he wasn't much of a outdoorsy guy. He could survive, because where he'd come from, you learned to do that early on. But he preferred the city. That jungle was his life's blood.

It was a clear night, and the sky was filled with stars. She set her plate on the blanket next to her, then leaned back and looked up at the sky.

He realized that when she wouldn't look at him was when she revealed the most about herself.

"Not that, so much as the whole date thing," she said at last.

"Why not?"

"My mother says it's because of my divorce."

She was divorced. He hadn't planned on his potential wife having been down the aisle once before.

He needed to find out more about this. "Is your mother right?"

She shrugged, took a sip of wine and stared at the openness around them. He realized she wasn't going to say any more. But he had big plans for her. And the bit of cleavage revealed by the neckline of her dress made it damned hard to concentrate on getting information about her past from her.

There was a sadness in her eyes that made him want to cradle her in his arms and promise that she'd never feel sad again. Of course, he knew that was a promise he couldn't keep, but still she made him want to take vows that would keep her safe. "What happened to end your marriage?"

"You don't want to hear about that."

"But I do. I'm very interested in everything that made you into the woman you are today."

"You don't have to try so hard."

He set his wineglass down, not sure he liked where this was going. He wasn't really trying hard to do anything except keep himself from touching her body and finding out if she really was as soft as he imagined. And from kissing her full lips to ascertain if they were as luscious as they looked.

"Try so hard at what?"

"Hitting on me," she said.

"Angel, you're not even close."

"I've heard that before." She crossed her arms

over and gave a look so prim it took all his will-power not to kiss it off.

He took a deep swallow of his wine and wished it was a double Scotch, instead. "No wonder you don't date."

"What do you mean?" she asked defensively.

"Exactly what you think it means. You're a pain in the ass."

"That's more like it," she said.

"What is?"

"Honesty. I know I've got more barriers than Nellis Air Force Base, but you have to understand that smooth talking is not going to turn my head."

"Why's that?"

"Because my ex-husband taught me a lesson about truth and men I'll never forget."

He didn't really want to hear about the other men in Kylie's life. Though he suspected there hadn't been many. She'd confessed to not dating, and there was a look about her that warned men away. He waited for her to go on.

She sighed and said, "Men are looking for something different than woman are."

"What is that?" he asked. He'd often wondered what women thought men were looking for. He also wondered about Kylie's ex-husband and what a fool the man must have been.

"A combination of Martha Stewart, Cindy Crawford and Madeline Albright," she said.

"And what do women want?"

"A woman wants to be loved for who she is. Not because of who a man wants her to be," she said quietly. She abruptly stood up and looked out at the vast landscape, and he knew she wasn't seeing the present but the past, and the woman she was and the man who couldn't love her. He vowed not to make the same mistake her ex-husband had.

Three

Deacon wasn't sure what kind of man her ex had been, but he knew he'd left Kylie with some pretty powerful delusions of what men wanted. Deacon was straightforward in his desires. The right lover made any woman feel like a supermodel. He made a mental note to prove to Kylie her desirability.

Love was a different matter. He'd learned early on that deep affection was an illusion. Every day he saw couples getting married in Vegas, couples swearing eternal devotion. A devotion that he suspected lasted only as long as they were in the make-believe land of casinos and nightclubs. A world apart from reality. He'd vowed at twenty-eight that he was through with love and he hadn't once gone back on his word. He didn't intend to.

"I'm not looking for any of those women you named, Kylie. Then again, I was raised around showgirls."

She tilted her head to the side and watched him. She was so shy sometimes and then at other times too bold. He had the feeling she was way out of her element here with him. He didn't know if that was a good thing or not.

"Was your mom a showgirl?" she asked.

He didn't want to talk about his past, but he also didn't want to lose Kylie because she thought he was like every other guy she'd ever met. If he knew one thing, he was nothing like those other men. Unless she'd frequented prisons. Only luck and determination had kept him from incarceration.

"Sort of."

"What kind of answer is that?"

An evasive kind that he'd hoped would satisfy her. But he should have known better. He wished he knew the right words to say. "She'd stopped performing by the time I came along."

"Did she quit working in the casinos?"

"Nah. She didn't know anything else. She started helping with costumes and makeup—that kind of thing."

"What about your dad?"

"Gone before I was born."

"Oh, I'm sorry."

"Don't be." He didn't regret not having a dad. He'd learned all he needed to know from Ricky the Rat when he was kid and then when he'd gotten older, he'd learned from Mac and others like him.

"You've always lived in Vegas?"

"Yes, I have." Honestly, he didn't think he could live anywhere else. It was in his blood. The twenty-four-hour world. New York and Los Angeles were okay to visit but too crowded for his tastes. The strip was busy, certainly, but it had a different sort of energy. The people in Vegas rejuvenated him.

Her eyes had lost that wounded look and for once he felt pretty good about himself. All this talking had helped her. "Where are you from?"

"Everywhere—my dad was career military. Growing up, we never lived in one place longer than three years."

"And now?"

"Since my divorce I've stayed put. I bought a little bungalow in Glendale, California, and planted a garden. I don't think I'll ever move."

"What if you get married?"

"I don't know. Like I said, I don't really date, so marriage doesn't seem much of an option."

The night breeze blew across the desert. Despite its warmth, she shivered a little, and he shrugged out of his suit jacket and draped it over her shoulders. She smiled her thanks, but her eyes were still guarded.

He didn't understand women and their need to label everything they felt, their need to analyze it to death, or at least that was what his mom did.

But he needed Kylie to trust him. Otherwise she'd never agree to be his wife. The moonlight painted shadows across the land.

He packed up the plates and cutlery and poured the last of the wine into Kylie's glass. She didn't take a sip, just toyed with the stem, rolling it between her fingers.

Her fingers were long and slender. He easily imagined her caressing him the same way she touched the wineglass. She licked her lips and scooted a little closer to him on the blanket.

"I have two questions," she said.

"Ask away," he said.

"Can I touch you?"

"Anywhere," he said. And meant it. His pulse had doubled as soon as the words left her mouth. And though he didn't plan for the first time he had sex with his respectable soon-to-be wife to be in the middle of the desert, he couldn't resist the notion of her hands on him.

Her fingers were cold when she touched his face. She cupped his jaw and rubbed the prickle of his five-o'clock shadow. He'd meant to take the time to shave again before they'd come out this evening, but time was always a premium in his business.

Kylie didn't seem to mind that he hadn't shaved. She lifted her other hand, completely framing his face. Her fingers moved with minute strokes against his skin, and shivers of awareness slithered down his spine and pooled in his groin.

He lifted his own hands, catching the back of her head and bringing her closer to him. He needed to taste her. Explore the feminine secrets that kept getting more mysterious the more time he spent with her.

He leaned forward, felt the brush of her breath against his skin. Her hands on his face were light and teasing. She watched him with wide eyes as she touched his skin and discovered the differences between them. He waited patiently until she thrust her hands into his hair, linked her fingers at the back of his head and urged him closer.

He needed no urging. He stopped thinking and simply reacted. She was woman to his man. And he'd already decided she should be his mate. There was nothing left to do but claim her.

He lowered his head the last few inches. A savagery ruled him and he tried to tame it, but couldn't. She was the embodiment of everything he'd been searching for in a woman, and here she was in his arms.

He took her mouth completely. Thrust his tongue

past the barrier of her teeth and tasted the heart of her. He pulled her across his lap so that he could have better access to her mouth. He slid one arm under her neck and shoulders and deepened the kiss even more.

With his free hand, he cupped her jaw and held her still for his complete domination. Her hands moved on him, stroking his jaw with a calming touch that talked to the beast inside him. The beast that had decided to claim her. The repeated strokes of her hands brought him back to himself and to her. He lifted his head. Her lips were swollen.

He needed to taste her again, but sanity raised its head, and he knew if kissed her again, he wouldn't stop until he was buried to the hilt in her luscious body. He tilted his head back, searching for control in the endless starlit sky and finding it only after he'd taken several deep breaths.

"You had another question," he said. He should set her aside, but not yet. He liked the feel of her soft curves against him, her rounded buttocks against his rock-hard thighs.

"What?" she asked. Knowing she was as dazed as he confirmed that he'd found the right woman to be his bride.

"You said two questions," he reminded her. He tucked her head under his chin and wrapped both arms around her.

"Why did you ask me out?"

"I'm attracted to you," he said bluntly.

"Is that all?" she asked.

He didn't know what she wanted from him. He knew that telling her he planned to marry her probably wasn't it. "Should there be more?"

"I'm a planner."

"I don't follow you, Kylie."

"I just want to know where this will lead," she said. She scooted away from him, and his arms felt empty without her. "I'm not really the vacation-fling kind of woman."

"I know," he said quietly. That was part of her attraction.

Silence grew between them. Deacon didn't have words to reassure her. Didn't know what she was trying to ask with her veiled questions. But he did know that if he pulled her back into his arms, he could reassure her in the most fundamental way a man could.

"You make me forget that," she said at last.

Her words were like a velvet glove on his groin. Hardening his arousal and strengthening his resolve to make her his. "Angel, sometimes your honesty is lethal."

"I can't be any other way," she said, twisting her hands together.

"Come here and let me hold you," he said.

"I'm not sure that's a good idea."

"I am."

"Deacon, I don't want to have sex with you out here."

"Well, hell. That kiss said otherwise."

"Which is why I'm backing off now. You make me forget things that are important."

He nodded and touched her face gently. Because she was so different from every other woman he'd ever dated, he forced himself to only brush his lips across her forehead. Shifting away, he said, "I'd never push you into something you weren't ready for."

I'd never push you into something you weren't ready for. The words echoed in her head, and she wondered how hard he'd have to push.

Kylie wanted to believe everything that Deacon said. And that was her first warning that her traitorous body had taken control. Her mind, her sensible mind, knew better than to give in to a smooth-talking guy with magic hands.

But there was something in Deacon's eyes that was different from Jeff's. A wildness to him that struck a chord in her soul. Tempting her with the knowledge that she could soothe him.

He made her feel desirable, something she hadn't felt in a long time. She hadn't been lying when she said she didn't date. Jeff had wounded the heart of her femininity when he'd tried to shape her into his idea of the perfect woman. And the men she'd gone out with immediately after her divorce had proved to be cut from the same cloth.

Deacon wasn't, though. She knew that with the wine and gourmet dinner he'd meant to seduce her under the stars. But his reaction to her touch had been instinctive, not part of any plan, she was certain.

She'd never been wined and dined before. Smooth jazz still poured from the speakers in his car. The night breeze had cooled a bit, Deacon's jacket and the man himself kept her warm.

This was a fantasy night, though she knew better than to buy into the whole illusion of it. The last time she'd believed in happily-ever-after, she'd ended up alone in a run-down duplex with more bills than money and shattered self-confidence. She wasn't going back to that place for anything, not even the incredible promise of pleasure in Deacon's arms.

Deacon was worlds different from her ex-husband, but he was still a man. She knew that for most men she represented a certain ideal woman. No one had ever bothered to look beyond the surface of her girl-next-door looks and sunny personality.

Deacon was different, though. His words. *His* honesty touched a spark deep inside her, and though she knew a vacation fling wasn't what she really wanted, a longing for him pulsed through her. She hated to fight herself. She wanted Deacon. Why was she making this so complicated?

She knew Tina was probably having sex with the guy she'd met in the casino earlier this afternoon. Tina had the most incredible vacation flings. But Kylie had never been able to compromise her standards enough to have an affair. She wasn't a prude. She didn't have to be married to sleep with a guy. She just wanted some reassurance that there was something more involved than just sex.

Deacon watched her with his brilliant gray eyes. Suddenly she felt as if everything she was thinking was broadcast on her face. Insecurity swamped her. She pulled the lapels of his jacket closer around her. God, she loved the way he smelled. She closed her eyes and breathed deeply. It was like being in his arms again. But a hundred times safer.

''I'm not sure what to say,'' she said at last. She definitely should have stayed in the room with her book. Her book was uncomplicated. Her book was easy to deal with. She knew her heart was going to ache when the foppish Percy Blakney got down on his knees and kissed the cobblestone where his estranged wife had just stepped.

But there was nothing predictable about Deacon. Even though being here with him tonight had a certain excitement, the potential for heartbreak was too great. She wished she'd never stepped out of her safe little world. From the moment she'd stepped on the plane to come to Vegas, she knew she'd taken unsound steps toward something new.

"Which part scared you?" he asked. He lightly traced his finger down the deep V left by his jacket. She shivered with awareness, realizing she'd been fighting her physical reaction to him because it was something she didn't know how to control.

"You have to know I want you," he rasped. Leaning forward, he cupped her face and dropped the lightest of kisses on her nose. Then he took her mouth in a kiss that was more intense than the one they'd shared earlier. While that one had been all about instinct and passion, this one was more profound, because of the way he controlled it. Actually, controlled himself and her. His mouth was thorough, leaving her feeling completely exposed to him. She slid her hands around his neck and held him tightly to her.

She took from the kiss what he offered. An intimate knowledge of himself and the kind of desire she'd never experienced with another man.

Her body had reacted to his words. Her breasts felt full and heavy and her nipples tightened, needing his hands and mouth on them. Her center was dewy. She shifted on the blanket, trying to get closer to him. He fell back, cradling her against him. She moaned deep in her throat. Oh, man, this was getting out of control. She needed him deep inside her. She ached for him.

He rubbed his hands down her back. A circular motion that applied pressure just where she needed it. He shifted them to their sides and then his left hand was cupping her breast. She tensed, waiting for his intimate touch on her aching flesh.

But he didn't caress her nipple. He only pulled her more fully into his body. She felt his erection nudge at her center and she wondered why he was gentling this embrace. He rocked them both side to side and then levered himself up off her.

"I—"

"Angel, I'd never hurt you," he said, cupping her jaw and running his thumb over her bottom lip.

"You can't control that," she said softly. "I'm the only one who can."

"Trust me," he said, his gravelly voice brushing over her senses.

Weak woman that she was, she was tempted to say whatever he needed to hear to keep him touching her. But she didn't.

Trust and honesty seemed to go hand in hand, but Kylie had found out the hard way that unless she really knew herself, her trust was fragile and effortlessly broken.

He continued running his finger over her bottom lip, and the touch was making her mindless. She pulled her head back and shook her head to clear it. "Trust isn't that easily won."

"Why not?" he asked bluntly.

For all his money and courtly manners, Deacon was at heart a very primal man. Though they hadn't known each other long, she'd come to realize that he used those smooth manners and his dry wit as a shield.

"Because trust is a bond. And it takes more than a few kisses to inspire it in me," she said. "It takes a long time for me to relax around anyone."

"It didn't seem that way a few minutes ago."

"Oh, Deacon. That wasn't trust."

He lifted one eyebrow, inviting her to go on. It was an imperious gesture, and she realized in that moment that Deacon was used to being in charge.

"That was pheromones and hormones. *Chemistry.* All men react to it."

"I'm not your ex-husband," he said quietly.

"I never thought you were. There's something in your eyes…a wildness…something untamed."

He glanced at her but didn't say a word. She wondered if she'd offended him.

Was she guilty of the same thing she'd been worried he'd do? Looking only at the surface image of successful casino owner and stopping there? From the little he'd told her of his past, she knew that he must have worked his way up the hard way.

But she was also sure that she was absolutely safe with him. He'd never hurt her or take advantage of her, and that perhaps was his greatest weapon in the battle she was waging against herself. She wanted to trust him. Already she was starting to.

"What man are you?" she asked, speaking more to herself than to him. He was so different from any other guy she'd ever met.

"The only man for you," he said, lowering his head again. The words filled a deep desire in her heart to be special to a man. His lips filled her soul with warmth and fire. She was tempted to believe him, even though she knew she wasn't the kind of woman for him.

Four

Deacon got them both back into the car before he lost complete control of the situation and made love to her in the one place he'd always felt the most comfortable. He switched off Louis Armstrong and found a hard-rock station. The raucous music of Creed filled the car, and Kylie surprised him by singing.

Deacon stepped on the gas. The wind ruffled their hair, and Kylie reached across the seat to rest her hand on his thigh. Her touch was tentative, not grasping, just something he imagined a married couple would do. It pleased him to know they were both on the same track. They'd be married in no time at all.

He already knew what he was going to use Mac's money for. One of those indoor playgrounds. The kind of place kids could explore for hours and still not discover everything.

"What was it like growing up in Vegas?" Kylie asked him. "We were stationed in Nellis one time, but I was only eight, so I couldn't come into the city."

"The same as anywhere else," he said. The last thing he wanted to talk about with Kylie was his past. Or himself. In fact, the less she knew about the real Deacon Prescott, the better it would be for all concerned.

"What was the same?"

He took her hand and brought it to his lips, brushing a kiss against her knuckles. "School and stuff."

"Deacon—"

"Tell me about yourself. Other than Nellis, where did you live as a child?" he asked, placing her hand back on his thigh and resting his hand on top of hers.

"Oh, San Diego, Germany, Florida. We lived everywhere. My older sister, Ramona—she's the smart one—calculated the miles in her head and she knows exactly how many we've traveled since birth."

"Do you have any other siblings?"

"Yes, there's Jessica. She's the pretty one. She always had tons of guys following her around. She made them build us an outrigger when we were in Hawaii.''

''Hmm…so Ramona's the smart one and Jessica's the pretty one. What does that make you?''

''The ordinary one.''

He realized that Kylie didn't realize that her own uniqueness was what made her special. ''You are many things, Kylie, but ordinary isn't one of them.''

''I…thanks, I guess.''

''Is this that blarney thing again?''

''It's just hard to believe what you're saying when I know the opposite is true.''

He vowed that even if the marriage thing didn't work out between them, he'd show Kylie Smith exactly how sexy and sweet she was. And he doubted that the smart and pretty sisters could hold a candle to her. Kylie changed the subject by telling him how Jessica's boys had spent five days building an outrigger.

He pulled into the valet line at the Golden Dream and motioned for the valet to wait until Kylie finished her story. Then Deacon turned off the car and they entered the hotel. He liked the way she talked about her family.

He had a strong feeling that her family was a close-knit one. And for a moment he felt a pang. But in the end it was another point in the wife column. She would know how to create the kind of family he craved.

He glanced at the lobby clock: ten minutes until midnight. He saw Angelo Mandetti talking to one of his dealers, who was on a break. He nodded to the older man to let him know he'd be with him in a few minutes.

"Just like Cinderella, I'm back before midnight," she said.

"I hope you'll leave me with more than a shoe." He pulled her out of the crowded lobby into a small alcove. There was a brocade love seat and a large tree that provided them some privacy.

"What do you want?" she asked.

He wanted a lot. More than he was prepared to ask for on their first date. He'd settle for a token. "Another one of those kisses of yours."

"Just one kiss," she said, tilting her head to the side. Her eyes were bright with excitement.

"For now." He leaned closer and took her mouth in a searing kiss, leaving a respectable space between them and letting his mouth show her all the things he wanted to do with her later.

She tasted of the wine they'd shared. Her hands came up and clung to his shoulders. He opened his eyes and saw that hers were closed. She held him tightly and stood on tiptoe to give him greater access to her mouth. He cupped the back of her head and angled his mouth over hers.

He thrust deeper into her mouth tasting the essence that was Kylie. God, it was addictive. He didn't want to stop. Hell, there was a sofa of sorts right here. He could settle her slight weight over his lap and let things move to their natural conclusion.

In fact, he would have if she'd been any other woman. If she hadn't been the woman he wanted for his wife, he would have taken her upstairs to his suite, instead of to this alcove.

He lifted his head.

"Oh, Deacon."

Oh, what? he wondered. But she said nothing else, just wrapped her arms around her waist and smiled at him with such sweet sincerity that he knew he was lost.

"I'll walk you to the elevators," he said.

"No. I'm meeting my friends in the bar."

"Then I'll escort you there."

"Thanks," she said. He cupped her elbow and led her through the lobby. Angelo Mandetti left the dealer and walked toward them.

Deacon introduced them.

"*Piacere, amico,*" Mandetti said.

"What language is that?"

"Italian. It means, 'Nice to meet you.'"

"Same here, Angelo."

"Kylie is meeting some friends in the bar," Deacon said. "Want to start our tour there?"

"Sounds good to me," Mandetti said.

They continued to the bar, Mandetti walking a

few paces behind them. Kylie scanned the crowded room and then bit her lip.

"What's wrong?" Deacon asked.

"They're not here. I think I'll head up to my room."

"Want to come with me?" he asked.

"I don't want to intrude."

"I'm just observing," Mandetti said.

"Then I'd love to," Kylie said with a smile.

Deacon tried not to let it matter that she'd been stood up by her friends. Or that he'd made her smile after she'd looked so sad. But it did matter, and not just because of the bet.

Kylie tried to tell herself that obviously Deacon was after only one thing. But she knew it wasn't true. As much as she didn't want to risk her heart again. As much as she knew that Vegas was the ultimate adult playground and she shouldn't buy into anything she saw here, as much as her mind told her otherwise, her heart was falling for the dark man with shadowed eyes.

"This is our main casino," Deacon said. "We have two rooms in the back that are visible from this floor for high-rolling poker games. Plus a few VIP rooms we keep on hand for whales."

"What's a whale?" Kylie asked.

"A high roller," Mandetti answered. "Usually

someone from out of town who has more money than he can spend in one week in Vegas.''

Kylie noted many similarities between Deacon and the older man. They moved the same way. A certain lightness on their feet that spoke of an ease with their bodies, combined with a self-confidence that other men saw as almost a dare.

''Do you gamble?'' Deacon asked.

''Not really. I played a few slot machines at the airport and in your lobby.''

Deacon said nothing, which she noticed was his way. He was very quiet and didn't reveal much of his life. All she really knew about him was that he'd grown up here and his mom had been a showgirl.

''This is roulette, right?'' she asked when they stopped near a green velvet table.

''Yes. Want to play?''

''I don't know how.''

''It's easy. I'll show you.''

He motioned to one of the uniformed employees that Kylie had observed earlier just standing around. The man came right over. ''We need some chips.''

He handed the young man five one-hundred-dollar bills and Kylie felt her reality shift again. She'd never had five hundred dollars in her pocket, and certainly never had the money to waste on a game.

''I'm not sure this is good idea. I'm really not that lucky.''

"I am," he said.

Mandetti laughed. The employee returned, handing Deacon a tray of chips. Guiding her with a hand on her waist, he pushed her through the small crowd gathered at the table until she had a front spot.

Deacon stood behind her, intimately pressed against her back. He set the tray on the table in front of her.

"The lady's feeling lucky, Ben."

"Ready to give the wheel a chance?" Ben asked.

Kylie had no idea. Deacon took a stack of chips from the tray. "What's your lucky number?"

"I don't have one," she said.

"Good thing I do."

Deacon placed the stack of chips on a black square with the number seven on it.

"Now what do we do?" she asked.

"Wait for the wheel and see if we hit pay dirt."

He stroked her arm and leaned over her shoulder, watching the wheel spin and the ball bounce and finally stop on a black square. She wasn't wearing her glasses, so she couldn't make out the number. But Deacon squeezed her arm and gave her a quick kiss, so she knew they'd won.

Ben placed an equal amount of chips next to the one Deacon had set out.

"Let it ride," Deacon said.

She leaned back against him and asked, "What's that mean?"

"Just that we're going to let our luck keep running."

"Does it work that way?"

"Sometimes."

"Isn't that risky?"

"No guts, no glory," he said.

The wheel spun again and they won a second time. Kylie knew their luck couldn't last, so she grabbed the chips before Deacon could let his bet ride again. "I think I understand the game now."

"What's the matter?"

"Nothing. I just don't want to owe you five hundred dollars."

"I would never take money from you."

"I don't want you to lose. You're lucky in things, Deacon. I'm not."

Deacon turned to Mandetti. "Can you give us a moment?"

"Sure. I want to watch Ben here for a few more minutes, and then I'm going to talk to the blackjack dealers."

Deacon took Kylie's elbow and led her across the room. There was a doorway marked Private, which he opened with a key card. The hallway was quiet and elegantly decorated. Everything around Deacon was first-class, she thought. She was uncomfortably aware that she'd carved a different kind of life for herself and wondered for a moment if Deacon would

have been interested in her away from this vaca-
tionland.

"Where are we going?"

"To my office. I want to talk to you away from
the crowd and the bells."

"About what?"

"About luck."

"What about it?"

"Only that you have to make luck, otherwise
you're liable to end up a bitter and lonely person."

"I think that's putting a lot of pressure on luck."

"I don't. Luck is what you make of it."

"Deacon, you don't need luck. You've got a
sheer force of will the likes of which I've never
encountered before."

"I'm glad you noticed," he said with a cocky
grin.

"Why's that?"

"Because there's something I want and I'm not
going to stop until I get it."

Normally Kylie would have been afraid to ask
him what he was talking about, but the look in his
eyes told her he was talking about her. Well, she
had decided to throw caution to the winds on this
trip, hadn't she?.

"Do you mean me?"

He flashed his key card once again and opened
the door to his office. They both entered. The room
was dimly lit and the lights of the pool were visible

outside the window. He tugged her into his arms, tipping her head back.

"Yes," he said, before lowering his mouth and kissing her.

"I thought we came here to talk," Kylie said.

He'd forgotten he'd lured her away from the casino with that promise. Actually he hadn't forgotten; he been sidetracked. He realized that a slow seduction was going to be more difficult than he'd planned. On one level, she was his future wife and he intended to treat her a certain way and to be that man he'd always wished he was. It was sobering to realize that no matter how much money he acquired, he was still that somewhat rough street kid.

"Yes, talk," he said. "I believe the topic was luck."

"I think we've explored luck enough for tonight. I want to know more about you."

"We've been over that. Come over here. Look, you can see our El Dorado. I think it's almost time for gold to cascade over the side."

"I saw it yesterday."

He said nothing, just remained where he was, staring out the window at the little world he'd created. He was the master here, and for all that Vegas and his life had always depended on the roll of the dice, he felt a certain sense of security and pride at the Golden Dream.

Kylie slipped her arm around his waist and leaned against him. He wanted her as his wife, but he didn't intend she ever know the details of his life and his past. There were boundaries he let no one cross—not even the woman he'd decided to marry.

"This isn't a good spot to really see the display. Come on. I'll take you to a special place I know you haven't seen."

"Deacon?"

"Yes?"

"I'm confused. I thought you wanted something from me."

"I do."

"Then why the diversion?"

He took a deep breath, sensing he was on the cusp of losing her. "There are certain parts of me that I share with no one."

"What parts?"

"My past. Please don't ask me about it again."

She said nothing, crossing her arms over her chest and tucking her chin down. He felt her shutting him out and didn't blame her. It might be the end to his plans and the loss of a bet. But he didn't want it to be.

"Should I escort you back to your room?" he asked. Defeat was foreign to him, so he wasn't giving up. Strategy was something he'd learned as a young man, and he knew when to retreat and regroup. If knowing about his past was going to be an issue between them, he'd tell her the story he told others who asked. The one he'd made up when he first started working in casinos, because few legitimate operations were interested in hiring a guy who'd worked in that shady gray area that was almost the other side of the law.

And Kylie was too innocent. There was something about her he wanted to protect. Even—especially—from himself.

She shook her head and let her arms fall to her sides. Crossing the room to him, she took his hand in hers and smiled at him. "I thought you were going to show me the hidden El Dorado."

He led her out of his office to a bank of elevators. They traveled quickly to the top of the building, and then he accompanied her through a glass-enclosed hallway that led to the other side of the resort. She paused and looked down on his kingdom and all of Vegas sprawled beyond.

Deacon stood next to her. This glass hallway was one of his favorite places. He could look out on the city he'd grown up in and see just how far he'd come. This was a view that the teenage Deacon had never had. And from up here the city seemed fun, exciting and clean. From the street he knew it was dirty and had an edge of excitement, but it came from wondering if you'd survive the night.

"I can't imagine growing up here," she said.

"Why not?"

"It just seems it'd be a hard place to live. Kind of like Jamaica. I visited there on a cruise last summer, and there was such a duality in the lifestyles. Wealthy cruise passengers buying stuff in town and the natives who made do with so little."

She'd hit it on the head. That was Vegas in one brief sentence. It was very important that she never realize that he'd been one of the natives.

He didn't say anything else, just took her elbow and led her back down the hallway. He loved touching her. Her skin was so soft and smooth. He knew she didn't need his hand on her arm to guide her, but he wasn't going to miss an opportunity to touch her.

He opened a door to a darkened staircase. He lifted her into his arms and carried her down the one flight of stairs quickly. When they reached the landing and viewing platform, he let her slide down his body. Keeping her in his arms, but turning her so that her back was pressed to his front. He lowered his head and whispered into her ear, "Prepare to be awed."

He couldn't resist nibbling at the smooth expanse of her skin by her ear. She shivered in his arms, her head falling back against his shoulder. He lifted his head and waited until the golden light of El Dorado filled the landing before taking her mouth in a kiss that asked for nothing. That took her completely with the intention of putting to rest any of the questions she might still want to ask.

Five

She knew in her heart that he was using the physical attraction that ran so strongly between them to distract her, but she didn't care. The darkness in Deacon's eyes spoke to her lonely soul. She needed to soothe him in whatever way she could.

But it wasn't only to soothe him that she lifted her arms and leaned more fully into his kiss. She kissed him to ease her battered heart, as well. Deacon touched a part of her she'd forgotten. The deep heart of her dreams that involved her ideas of life, love and forever after.

She sighed, opening her eyes to look at him. His eyes were open and he watched her with an intensity that shook her. She pulled back.

He said nothing, just continued to watch her with the gaze that reaffirmed what he'd stated earlier. He wanted her. He wasn't giving up until he had her.

She had to be honest. She was excited and flattered that he thought she was worth the struggle. But another part of her, the wounded part, wondered if she could live up to what he'd expect from her.

She cupped his face, rubbing her fingers against the stubble on his chin. "Don't expect too much from me."

In reply he lowered his head and took her mouth again. Thought fled and she surrendered herself to him completely.

He tasted good and spicy. A familiar taste on her tongue now. Behind him rained liquid gold. It was incredibly beautiful and lent the entire episode a dreamlike feeling.

She shivered, sliding her hands down to his shoulders. They were so broad she felt tiny by comparison. Even though she'd never been petite.

His hands on her waist pressed her into his body as he deepened the kiss. She opened her mouth to his thrusting tongue. He eased one thigh between her legs and she rubbed herself against him. Her breasts felt full and heavy and her nipples tightened.

He moaned deep in his throat and moved one hand slowly upward. His touch was measured, stopping beneath her right breast. He just held her, one hand burning through the fabric of her dress at her waist, the other filling her with anticipation that at any moment his fingers might move farther and her aching nipple would receive his attention.

Deacon seemed to have all the time in the world and was interested in only exploring her mouth. Taking his time to learn all her secrets. She realized she was passively lying in his arms. Letting Deacon, with his strong will, mold her as he would.

She lifted her hands from his shoulders and shoved her fingers into his hair, then held his head while she took control of the kiss. She had little experience with men. Her ex had been very aggressive and liked it best when she just let him do everything. But she mimicked Deacon's actions. He'd made her feel cherished and sexy and she yearned to evoke the same feelings in him. Hungry and needing something that only Deacon could provide her.

She kept her eyes open. Noticed that his had narrowed and the hands that had been resting so patiently only moments before started to move. His hand under her breast moved to cup its fullness, then rubbed the globe with a light teasing circular motion.

She undulated against him until his palm was right over her nipple. He lifted his head, looking down at her with eyes that glowed with primal need. His lips were swollen from their kiss.

She felt pulses of awareness shuddering through her. Heat pooled low in her belly, and she wanted nothing more than to push him to the ground and fall on top of him.

Before she could act or speak, Deacon lifted her and pivoted to rest against the wall. She grasped his biceps as he lifted her higher and pulled her closer.

"Put your legs around my waist."

She did as he asked. A minute later she felt his mouth on her nipple through the material of her bra and dress. She shuddered again, rocking against him. She felt helpless in her passion. And totally under his command.

She grabbed his head and held him to her breast. He suckled strongly and then scraped his teeth over her aroused flesh. She squirmed against him, needing more than he was giving. He switched his attention to her other breast, which intensified the ache between her legs.

She tunneled her fingers through his thick dark hair and held him to her as he suckled her breast. Each pull of his lips and touch of tongue sparked an answering pull deep in her center. She tried to tighten her legs, but he was there between them.

She rocked against his hard middle seeking something she couldn't find there.

"Deacon," she gasped.

He raised his head, then took her hips in his hands and shifted her on his body. He held her still until his penis nudged the center of her body. Exactly where she needed to feel his hardness. They fit together well.

She reached between their bodies, caressing him through the fabric of his pants. His hips jerked forward under her touch and she reached for his zipper. Lowering it, she slipped her hand into his trousers.

His hands slipped under her dress, rubbing her through her panties. The fabric between her legs was already damp with need. Deacon lowered his head to hers again and, still teasing her feminine flesh, whispered words of passion in her ear. Then he slipped one finger beneath her cotton panties and touched her.

She gasped his name again. His touch was sure and knowing, and was where she needed it most. She rubbed against him. He nibbled on the length of her neck, settling at the base and suckling her there.

She'd never felt so on fire before. She grasped his shoulders, held on for dear life as he rocked against her aroused flesh, not entering her, just letting her ride his length. Then she felt every nerve in her body tensing and tightening, and her climax broke over her in waves. She clung tighter to Deacon, held his head in her hands and closed her eyes.

He held her with arms that were tender and gentle as she returned to herself. He slid her down his body so that she was standing on her own feet and leaning against him. His erection nudged her belly and she realized he hadn't come with her.

She reached for him, intending to return the favor. But then his cell phone rang. He cursed savagely under his breath, released her and paced away.

His phone continued ringing. He braced his hands on the glass window through which the golden light had been shining. The light was gone now, leaving only the distant glow of the hotel lights. He leaned his head against the glass. His eyes were closed and his breath was coming in harsh pants.

The phone was a reminder of a world she'd forgotten existed. This place now was a fantasy world, and Deacon Prescott wasn't a man who'd be happy with the kind of girl Kylie Smith was.

Deacon reached down to adjust himself and zip his pants before answering his phone. He listened to his duty manager explain that they had a couple of con men in the security office. It wasn't something that Deacon could ignore.

But he wanted to. He was still hard, and only the thought of carrying Kylie upstairs to his bedroom had kept him from entering her moist body moments earlier.

"I'm sorry, angel, but I've got to go take care of a problem."

Her lips were swollen from his kisses. Her nipples still stood out against the bodice of her dress, and her hair was mussed. He didn't want to leave her. For the first time since he'd begun his quest to be the ruler of his own kingdom, he resented that kingdom.

"I know you have a business to run," she said.

He wanted to ask her to wait for him but it was late; just because he only needed four hours' sleep to function didn't mean that Kylie did.

"I'll walk you back to your room," he said.

He wanted to see her safely to her bed. To tuck her in and make sure she was safe before he went back to his world.

"That's not necessary."

"It is to me," he said, cupping her elbow and leading her down the hallway. The corridor was still dark. He knew he should carry her up the stairs, but didn't trust himself to take her in his arms again. He wanted her too badly.

Even standing this close to her was torture. The scent of her filled his nostrils, and it took all his willpower not to lower his head and breathe in the scent of her.

"Careful," he warned, guiding her with a hand on her back as they climbed the steps.

He stopped her at the top of the stairs. The well-lit landing showed that her skin was still flushed and her pupils were still dilated. Her breathing was shallow. He pulled her close to him, realizing he'd moved too fast for her. She'd warned him earlier, but he'd never been good at not reaching out and taking what he wanted.

He should apologize. Dammit, tonight was supposed to have been a slow seduction. Too bad his body had other ideas.

He cradled her face in his hands and tipped her head back. He couldn't say the words he knew a gentleman would say. The words that perhaps a guy like Mac, who'd grown up in a world where women were different, might. The words that would somehow magically make their encounter, which hadn't lasted long enough, seem right.

So instead, he kissed her. Showing her with his body that she was precious to him. Making promises he knew she wouldn't recognize or understand. He sipped at her lips with a restraint he was amazed he had.

When Kylie slid her arms around his waist, he knew he had to pull away, stop this before it went any farther. He was being noble here, and she needed to understand that right now he was all illusion. He was playing to her image of what a gentleman should be.

He held both her hands in his. She watched him with eyes that were wide and hungry, and again he cursed the very thing that had enabled them to meet—the Golden Dream.

"Why don't I wait in your office for you?" she said.

"No."

She stepped back as if he'd slapped her. Crossing her arms, she raised one eyebrow at him. He'd forgotten her feisty side and knew he was about to become reacquainted with it.

"I thought we had some unfinished business," she said.

"Not tonight. I want it to be right for you, angel."

He wanted to continue the discussion with her but didn't. He opened the door leading to the executive offices and Kylie followed him reluctantly.

"I don't want to be sent off to my room. I'm going back to the bar to find my friends."

"Kylie, don't—"

"Don't what?"

He had no answer for her. He wasn't going to tell this sweet woman that she made him feel weak in ways he'd never felt before.

"That's what I thought. I guess this is goodbye."

"No, it's not."

"Then what is it?"

"It's good-night."

She gave him a half smile, then fluffed her hair and started down the hall. He knew she didn't understand why he was sending her away. Hell, he didn't, either. It was just that he wanted everything to be perfect for her.

"Angel?"

She glanced over her shoulder at him. His breath

caught in his chest, and he wanted something he'd never wanted before. Not money, which seemed to come to him easily once he'd understood the order of the world. Not acceptance from society, which still eluded him, but the longing to be her hero. To have that woman look at him with respect because he'd earned it, not because he'd surrounded himself with the trappings of wealth.

"I want our first time to be memorable," he said at last.

She walked back toward him, her hips swaying with each step she took. How could he ever have thought this woman was meek and shy?

She stopped when barely an inch of space separated them. Every nerve in his body was acutely aware that he could lift her up and carry her to one of the empty offices along this hall and take her.

Standing on tiptoe, she braced her hands against his shoulders and whispered right into his ear, "How could it be anything but memorable?"

He shuddered as she gently bit his earlobe and walked away. Any doubts he had about Kylie being the perfect candidate for his wife disappeared, and he knew without a shadow of a doubt he'd met his match. This ride was going to be a wild one.

Kylie awoke the next morning to the sun streaming in the windows and a note propped in front of the clock. It was from Tina.

Hey, roomie! Going biking (Harley!) with Bob today. Catch you in the lounge at 7 tonight for drinks. Sorry about last night.

Kylie stretched and dropped the note back on the nightstand. She'd dreamed of Deacon all night. Erotic dreams that continued the lovemaking they'd started under the waterfall. She ran her hands down her body, remembering his touch.

She'd played another game of roulette before heading up to her room. It hadn't been the same without Deacon pressed to her back, and she'd lost. It drove home the fact that everything in this town changed on a dime. She'd be wise to remember that. To remember that anything between Deacon and her was only fleeting.

She'd never had a vacation fling before. Never contemplated having sex with a man she'd never see again when she returned home. In fact, what they'd done under the El Dorado waterfall was the farthest she'd gone with sex since Jeff. But it didn't bother her. She felt as if she was awakening as the woman she was meant to be with Deacon.

She pushed the covers off the bed and stood. The message light was flashing on her phone.

The message was from Deacon, his dark voice bringing every nerve ending to tingling awareness. He invited her to breakfast in his suite at nine.

It was twenty minutes after nine. She'd never

been a morning person, and she usually had a hard time dragging herself out of bed for work. She bit her lip. Should she keep her distance from Deacon?

She dialed the private number he'd left on the message. He answered on the third ring.

"Prescott."

"It's Kylie."

"Good morning, angel."

"Morning. Is your breakfast invitation still good? I just got up."

"How about if we change it to brunch? I'll be in meetings until eleven."

"If you're busy, we can do it another time."

"I'm not."

She needed to get it together, except that Deacon made her feel very...not like herself. She'd always thought she was the steady and predictable one. But Deacon made her want to be...wild.

"Where should I meet you?" she asked. She'd hoped to have time to explore the hotel a little. The resort's theme was "all things Golden," according to the pamphlet in her room.

"I'll come to you. What are your plans for the morning?"

"I thought I'd go to the pool to read."

"I'll join you there."

"I'll have to change clothes if we're going to eat." She didn't want him to see her in her old granny bathing suit, complete with skirt. Any woman who was going to be a mate to a man like Deacon would wear a bikini or something sexy.

"No, you won't. I'll arrange for brunch in my suite."

She'd go shopping in the hotel. Surely it had a clothing boutique. She'd need something sophisticated. "Okay."

"Good. I'll see you then," he said, and disconnected.

Kylie wasted no time getting dressed and hurrying downstairs to the lobby. Sure enough, off one hallway was a boutique that sold swimsuits in a rainbow of colors and selections, all with matching bath scarves. She was deliberating between a cobalt-blue one and a safer, more conservative black suit.

"The blue brings out your eyes," a man said behind her.

She glanced over her shoulders planning to move away without a word, but realized it was Mr. Mandetti, whom she'd met last night.

"Hello, Mr. Mandetti."

"Just Mandetti."

"Not Angelo?" she asked.

"God, no. That's someone's idea of a joke."

A silence fell between them. It was the kind of awkward moment she was used, to though she doubted that anyone who didn't have her terminal shyness ever experienced it. She remembered the tip that Tina had given her long ago. Ask about work.

"So does the gaming commission keep an eye on the merchandise operations, as well?"

"Normally, no. I came in for some pain medication."

He held up a small bag bearing the hotel's logo. "Do you mind some unsolicited advice?"

"I guess not."

He took the two tank styles she'd chosen and put them back on the rack. He pushed some suits aside and pulled out a bikini in a tropical print. Then he pulled out a matching red scarf and handed them both to her.

"This is something that Deacon will want to see on you."

It seemed odd to be having this conversation with a man old enough to be her father. But there was masculine knowledge in his eyes, and she knew he was right.

Before she could change her mind, she checked the sizes and went to the register to pay.

Mandetti winked at her as he walked out of the shop. *"Ciao, amico."*

"Bye, Mandetti."

She wondered if Deacon would recognize the signals she sent him. It wasn't as if this was the first time she'd ever tried to seduce a guy, but this was the first time it had really mattered. And that scared her way more than anything ever had before.

Six

Deacon knew that he shouldn't use the security cameras as a tool to aid in his seduction but he'd been unable to resist stopping by the security room to check on Kylie. He'd seen her in the boutique purchasing a swimsuit. He'd watched Mandetti talk her into one that he knew was going to look exquisite on her slender frame. And he'd debated the merits of skipping his meeting to join her early.

In the end he'd opted for business. Kylie was important and he didn't intend to ignore her, but he had a strategy. And part of that strategy was to make her want him with the same intensity he wanted her.

Of course, it was a double-edged sword, and he

was uncomfortably aware of the cut of his pants as he sat in the meeting imagining Kylie lying in the sun and waiting for him. Finally he could stand it no longer, and he ended the meeting fifteen minutes early.

He doubled-checked with Martha to make sure his orders had been carried out before leaving to meet Kylie by the pool. He saw Mandetti on the floor and stopped to talk to him.

Mandetti reminded him of a guy his mom had dated when he was about twelve. For some reason Marco had never dismissed him and had taken time to talk to him. There was a slight physical resemblance between the two men, but what really struck Deacon as similar was their eyes. In Mario and Mandetti's eyes Deacon saw the same thing he'd observed in his own shaving mirror.

It was a cold and bleak place where he and these two other men existed. A place without commitment or family. A place that Deacon sincerely hoped to leave by marrying Kylie.

''Mandetti, how's things?''

''Eh, *compare*. Things are good. I like your operation. Makes me wish I'd wised up a few years sooner than I did and gotten into this kind of thing.''

''What'd you do before?''

''You don't want to know.''

''I know where you're coming from,'' Deacon said.

Mandetti nodded. "I saw your lady earlier."

"I noticed."

"Keeping close tabs on her?"

Deacon shrugged, feeling a little foolish.

"She's shy," Mandetti said. "How's the bet going?"

"I'll win. I never lose when I set my mind to it."

"I'm rooting for you."

Mandetti's cell phone rang and he turned away to take the call.

Deacon made his way through the casino out to the pool. In the distance was the huge structure they called El Dorado. It was an Aztec-like structure with a huge waterfall that even during the day had plumes of water that turned gold every fifteen minutes. It had cost more than Deacon had wanted to spend on a water display, but he'd learned from Mac that the more you invested in your resort, the higher the profits down the road.

He paused at the bar to order a Scotch for himself and a strawberry margarita for Kylie. He spotted her lounging in the sun. Her chair was pulled a distance away from those around her. She wore large sunglasses and her dark hair was pulled back in a ponytail. Her book was in her hand, and Deacon knew he would have to work hard to make a place for himself in Kylie's world. She was very self-contained.

He didn't dwell on his doubts. He fixed an image

of Kylie in his head where before a faceless woman had been. Kylie would be his wife. Things had progressed too far for him to pick anyone else. At least that's what he told himself. He didn't want any other woman.

He moved across the pool deck, intent on Kylie. She was an island of calm amidst the chaos that was Vegas. People were talking and laughing. Smoking and drinking. Kissing and fighting. And there, apart from them, sat the woman he'd chosen for his own.

He didn't feel worthy of her, and he hoped she'd never realize how little in this life he'd done right. Last night he'd come close to lying about his past. She was just too innocent of life in general for him to contemplate telling her the truth.

"May I join you?" he asked.

She glanced up at him over the rims of her sunglasses. The smile that broke over her face was tentative. Did she have doubts about him already?

"Sure," she said, glancing around for a vacant lounger. There were none.

He lowered himself onto her lounger by her thighs. They were smooth and tanned and, he knew from last night, strong. He handed the margarita to her and took a stiff swallow of his own drink. Tried to remind himself that they were in public and he should keep his hands to himself.

He studied her in the sunlight. Last night in the shadows he'd become acquainted with her body, but much of it was still a mystery to him. Her tropical-print bikini left little to the imagination. The top lovingly hugged the full curves of her breasts. Her trim midriff was bare, and her bikini bottom was barely visible beneath the translucent red cover-up she'd wrapped low on her hips.

He hardened in his pants and knew that lunch was going to be a very quick meal—he didn't think he could draw out this seduction much longer.

"Did your meetings finish early?" she asked.

Clearly she wasn't on the same track. He took another swallow of his Scotch, trying to quench the desire pulsing through him with each breath he took. Each breath that was filled with her unique feminine scent. Each breath that felt hotter than the one before.

"Yes," he said when he realized she was staring at him.

"Thanks for the drink," she said. He watched her take a delicate sip and then lick her lips. God, she was killing him.

He rested his hand on his leg and knew if he moved his fingers the slightest bit to the left, he'd be touching her. He wasn't a subtle guy. He downed the rest of his Scotch and gave his empty glass to a passing waiter.

Hands free, he was able to caress her the way he'd been wanting to. He traced a random pattern on her thigh and was rewarded when she shifted her legs under his touch. Not out of his reach but into his caresses.

"Are you ready for brunch?" he asked, needing to get out of this very public area because the things he wanted to do with her were very private.

"Yes," she said. Her husky voice shot right through him, and he reached for her hand to help her to her feet. He knew that nothing had been decided, but when he slipped his arm around her waist to lead her back to the hotel, he had the feeling that everything was coming up sevens and he was riding a winning streak that couldn't be broken.

Kylie was acutely aware of Deacon's hand on her waist as they walked toward the hotel. Even though the pool area was busy and noisy, she was totally focused on the man next to her. Her pulse pounded in her ears and heat pooled low in her belly.

She leaned closer to him as they walked and felt his hand dip lower on her waist, resting on her buttocks. She shivered in purely sensual awareness. She'd never thought of herself as sex-crazed, but no less than twenty-four hours after meeting Deacon Prescott, she could easily see herself becoming just that.

The man exuded sexuality the way other men exuded power or wealth. There was something so purely masculine in his eyes that it called forth everything feminine in her. It made her want to preen and toss her hair. To switch her hips and send out every signal she knew that said, *Take me, big boy.*

The sun had warmed her through and through, leaving her feeling almost lazy with lassitude But it was tinged with the excitement she'd only experienced with him. An excitement that was quickly waking every nerve ending.

"I tried the roulette table without you," she said to distract herself from the memory of how those lips of his had felt under hers last night. God, she wanted to kiss him again. Instead, she was playing a waiting game. She'd always been a good girl, a rule follower, and that had never bothered her until now.

"How'd you do?" he asked. He maneuvered her through a crowd of college-age kids near the bar, protecting her from a wildly gesturing young man. Deacon put his arm around her and hugged her close for a minute. The guy gave them a halfhearted apology, and they moved on.

She savored the moment resting her head on his strong shoulder. It had been a long time since she'd even thought about letting a man into her life.

"Did you win?" he asked.

"No. I didn't do very well without you. I think you must be my good-luck charm."

"That's a first."

"I thought you believed in fate and luck."

"I do for me, but I've never brought it to someone else."

"Well, you did for me."

He appeared unaware that he'd used his body as a shield for her, but she tucked the knowledge away. As they neared the hotel, he directed her to a shady grotto hidden from the main path. There was a small bench beside a water fountain.

She looked at him questioningly.

"I wanted a few minutes alone with you before we're immersed in the crowd," he said. He pulled her into his arms again and lowered his head, taking her mouth in the sort of kiss she'd been craving from the moment he'd arrived at her lounger with drinks.

She tipped her head to the side to allow him deeper access. She stood on tiptoe, pressing her breasts against his chest and shivering as his big hands slid up her back. He slipped one finger under the fastening of her bikini top and caressed the skin between her shoulder blades.

She ran her hands up his chest and knotted her fingers behind his neck. Holding on to him gave her the illusion of control. With tentative sweeps of her tongue, she tasted him. He was patient, letting her set the tone of the kiss until she tickled the roof of his mouth with her tongue.

He groaned deep in his throat and leaned back against the low rock wall surrounding the grotto. Cradling her against his hips, he lifted his head. His lips glistened from their kiss and she lifted her hand to wipe away the moisture.

"Is this what you had in mind when you invited me to brunch?"

"More or less. I'd forgotten what a temptation you are."

"It must be this new swimsuit."

"Did you buy it for me?" he asked.

She nodded. She wasn't used to doing things for men. Her independence meant standing on her own two feet. It also meant doing things that pleased only her.

"Model it for me."

She stepped away and held her arms out from her sides, then spun slowly.

"I can't see your legs."

She had the scarf wrapped around her waist. Even out in the pool she'd kept her legs covered. In the privacy of her own backyard, she sunbathed with her legs exposed, but in public kept her legs covered. She hated the way her hips looked. Her mother always said, she'd have no trouble birthing babies with those hips.

"I've got secretary spread," she said.

He arched one eyebrow, but said nothing. Finally she sighed and untied the scarf from where it rested on her hips. She held the fabric open and watched his eyes narrow as her body was revealed to him.

"Turn again," he said. She let the fabric slide

from one hand to trail on the ground as she slowly pivoted. She stopped when her back was toward him, glancing over one shoulder.

His skin was flushed and his eyes were narrowed as he watched her. "Damn."

"What's the matter?"

"I wanted to get to know you today."

"And now you think you won't be able to?"

"I don't want to do anything but get you naked."

She trembled, hearing the intent in his voice. She turned back toward him. "I'm only in Vegas four more days."

"Do you object?"

"I probably should."

"Come on," he said.

They entered the casino. The air was cool and she shivered a little as her body adjusted to the temperature. Mandetti was waiting for Deacon as they stepped inside.

He gave her a look of approval. "Nice suit."

"Thanks," she said with a smile.

Deacon watched the interchange but said nothing. She noticed he tended toward silence.

"What can I do for you, Mandetti?" Deacon asked.

"Sorry, *compare*. I've got my director breathing down my neck. I need to see the safe and talk to you about your deposit information."

"We were on our way out for brunch. Would you like to join us?" Deacon asked.

Huh? She'd thought that Deacon was planning to seduce her in his suite. At the very least, she'd hoped to maybe seduce him. She'd even shaved her legs and dabbed expensive perfume on all of her pulse points in hopes of not smelling sweaty after lying in the sun.

"I don't want to interrupt your plans," Mandetti said.

"We'd be honored to have you join us. Kylie wants to know about the casino business."

"I do," she said. "I was asking Deacon about it last night. I've never had the opportunity to see the inner workings of a hotel/casino before." That much was true. And Deacon did have a job to do. She might be on vacation, but he wasn't. Just once she wanted to mean more to a man than his career did. But she cut Deacon some slack considering she'd known him only for a day.

"What do you do?" Mandetti asked.

"I'm a secretary at an ad agency in Los Angeles," she said. She thought about her job at Leiberman and Vox. She liked working for the VP, and it kept her busy most days. But it wasn't very rewarding; it wasn't her life, the way she sensed Deacon's casino was for him.

"Do you like it?" Deacon asked.

"Most days. But it's just a job."

"Let's go up to my quarters," he said to Mandetti. "I've arranged a cold buffet to be brought there."

"I'll join you in a few minutes, Deacon," Kylie said.

"Why?" he asked.

She needed a few minutes to herself before spending any more time in his presence. She couldn't switch gears as quickly as he did. And Deacon might approve of her body in this bikini, but she didn't savor the idea of eating in front of Mr. Mandetti in only her swimsuit.

"I'll give you two a few minutes," Mandetti said, walking toward the executive hallway.

"What's up, Kylie?"

"Nothing. I just want to change."

"You look fine."

"I'm not comfortable."

Deacon nodded. Without another word he escorted her to the guest elevators. He pressed the button for her floor and rode up with her, not saying a word.

"Someday, angel, you will be comfortable, I promise you," he said, kissing her as the doors opened.

"Go change. I'll wait here for you."

She nodded and headed down the hall in a daze. Deacon rattled her on so many levels. And she realized she didn't mind in the least.

* * *

Mandetti had arrived just in time, Deacon thought, to keep him from blowing it with Kylie. He'd taken a cold shower last night and another one this morning, but still he knew nothing short of being buried hilt-deep in Kylie's body was going to provide any relief.

And he'd vowed to let things develop slowly between them. But that had been before he'd realized that she was temptation incarnate and all of his fine plans for a wife and no premarital sex had gone out the window.

He'd only made the plan because it had seemed gentlemanly, even though the idea of it had gone against the grain. And he knew Kylie wasn't waiting for a ring. Hell, she didn't even know he planned to marry her.

The eighteenth floor had been decorated in hues of gold. In fact, every floor was decorated in some shade of gold. The wing in which Kylie's room was located was dedicated to the legends of gold from ancient Greece. On one wall there was a hanging of a replica of the mythical Golden Fleece that Jason had successfully sought. He leaned against the wall and studied it.

He wondered sometimes what it said about him that he had only copies of mythical and valuable things. He knew it was a direct correlation to his own life in which he pretended to be a wealthy guy.

One to whom things like thousand-dollar suits and fancy sports cars were taken for granted. But in his heart he was still a street fighter and he didn't take anything for granted.

Not even Kylie. Especially not Kylie. He needed to woo her. Not seduce her. And though it was hard as hell to keep his cool, he knew he had to. He wanted her to accept his marriage proposal before she flew home. He didn't even have the two weeks that he and Mac had bet on. He had four days.

She reentered the hall wearing a sundress similar to the one she'd had on the day before. Demure and not the least bit flirtatious. The skirt was respectable, reaching to the tops of her knees. Yet all he could see was her slim body covered in only that brief bikini.

"Sorry I was so long. Tina called to say she won't be back tonight."

"Good, then you're free for dinner with me."

"I'd like that," she said.

He slipped his hand under her elbow and led her back to the elevators. The car was empty when they got on. Deacon made himself step away from her. Hell, she smelled good. Like flowers first thing in the morning.

No other woman of his acquaintance smelled like her. His mom and her pals had always smelled of Chantilly. And the women he'd dated recently had used something that had undoubtedly cost top dollar, but it hadn't affected him half as much as Kylie's simple smell of spring flowers.

"I was surprised when you invited the gaming commissioner to join us for lunch," she said at last.

"Things are moving too fast for us. I don't want to rush. And Mandetti makes an interesting chaperon." Some classical music was playing in the background of the elevator. He liked the air it lent the casino, even though personally he couldn't stand the stuff. He'd rather have some spicy jazz, but he knew most of his guests felt more pampered with classical music in the background.

"I'll say. Are you sure that's it? Or did you change your mind once you saw my body?"

He cursed savagely under his breath. And hit the elevator stop button. Her eyes widened as he closed the gap between them, caging her between his body and the mahogany wall of the car. Her widened eyes watched him, and Deacon was aware that he'd slipped the reins of his control once again. Something he couldn't seem to avoid doing when Kylie was near.

"The only thing I thought when I saw your body was how quickly could we get to my room."

"Promise?"

He lowered his head, brushing kisses against her shoulder where the strap met her soft skin. He turned her in his arms until they both faced the mirror on the back wall of the elevator car.

She looked so damned right in his arms. How could she be blind to that?

He normally kept his thoughts to himself. He didn't like to let anyone inside his head. But in Kylie he found a kindred spirit. She'd been battered by life in a different way than he had. And he knew he could reassure her on this count.

"When I look at you, angel, I see the most beautiful woman in the room."

"Yeah, right."

"Be quiet," he said. "Your hair's so thick and soft it reminds me of the finest sable. I can't wait to bury my hands in it. To feel it against my skin." He lifted a strand of her hair and brought it to his face. Rubbed it over his lips and nose.

"Your eyes are deep bottomless pools that fascinate me. Sometimes everything you feel is revealed in them, but mostly, they hide your secrets. I'll do whatever is necessary to make you reveal them to me."

"I don't have any secrets. I'm just a plain ordinary girl from California."

"No, you're not. Your body is the stuff dreams are made of."

He caressed her elegant neck, brushing her hair to the side to drop a kiss at its base. She shuddered in his arms, and he pulled her more firmly against his body. His skin felt too tight. But he'd started this and he intended to finish it.

He cupped her breasts through the fabric of her dress. Her nipples budded against his palms and his body answered by tightening. "Your breasts are—"

"Too small."

"Just right," he said, rubbing his palms in wide circles until she shifted against him.

He slid his hand down her stomach, lingering right above her sex. "This part is full of mystery. I want to spread you out on my bed and take my time discovering what touches you like."

"I'm sure I'd like all your touches."

"Don't say things like that. We have lunch to get through."

"Then you better stop—"

"But I'm not done yet."

She crossed her arms. "Please don't look at my legs again."

"I'm going to. They fascinate me. I'm obsessed with thinking about their length and how they'll feel wrapped around my hips when we're both naked and twisting on the sheets together."

She trembled and lifted her eyes to meet his. "Deacon, where have you been all my life?"

"Just a roll of the dice away," he said with levity he was far from feeling. He radioed his office and had them tell the commissioner he was indisposed this afternoon. Kylie said nothing, but he knew she read the intent in his eyes as he put his hand in the center of her back and walked her down the long hall to the elevators that led to his private retreat.

Seven

Deacon's living quarters were spacious and state-of-the-art, a blending of elegance and comfort. Much like the man himself. The foyer was decorated with antiques that Kylie knew her mom would adore. The floor was Moroccan tile, and original artwork hung on the walls. He hit a button on the wall of the living room, and the window blinds opened to reveal the city of Las Vegas spread out beyond.

There was a bar in one corner of the living room, a large pool table in the middle and two separate sitting areas, one facing the windows, the other facing a top-of-the-line entertainment center. Pool was her dad's game and she'd learned to play at his side.

"This is really nice," she said inanely. She'd wanted to come with him. Wanted to make love with him. But at this moment she was nervous. Despite his reassurances in the elevator, she knew what she looked like when she was naked and laying on her back. Her boobs weren't big enough to look like much when she was horizontal. And Deacon…well, Deacon was the kind of guy that was solid muscle. She was realistic enough to know that making love in the bright light of day was going to leave her vulnerable.

"I hired a decorator to do it. The only thing that's mine is the pool table. Do you play?"

"Not in the last few years."

"You didn't think you'd be good at roulette, either," he said in a low voice.

She remembered the feel of him pressed against her back. Remembered his arms around her as he placed the bet. Remembered the excitement of trying something new and of having him by her side encouraging her to be more adventurous than ever before. She liked this new woman. And decided then and there to stop letting her fears rule her life.

"I was only good with you by my side," she said. The words resonated inside her, and she knew she was falling for Deacon Prescott, no matter that she'd known him only a short time. Her body and her soul said he was the one for her.

He crossed to the pool cues on the wall and took two down. "Wanna play?"

"Sure," she said, reaching for one of the cues. Wouldn't he be surprised when she learned she was a skilled player? After her dismal performance at roulette, she was looking forward to doing something that made her look good.

"Want to make things interesting?" he asked. The devilish gleam in his eyes made her pulse quicken.

"A bet?" she asked. In her heart she knew she should tell him she was very good at this game, but she wanted to see how far he was going to take this.

"Yes."

"What did you have in mind? I'm not in your league—I can't drop five hundred dollars and not worry about it."

"Why don't we play for something you won't mind dropping?"

"I'm listening," she said. She didn't trust that gleam in his eyes. He moved around the table so that they stood side by side. He rested his hip on the pool table.

"Clothes?" he said with a nonchalance belied by the narrowing of his eyes and the straining body part in his trousers.

"Strip pool?"

"Kind of. But you can wager items of clothing.

Say, for example, you wagered your panties and lost. You'd still be clothed.''

''Hmm. The loser takes off an article of clothing at the end of each game?''

''I was thinking we could bet on the sinking of each ball.''

She bit her lower lip. ''You're on. By the way, I want your pants first.''

''Why?''

''So I can ogle your legs,'' she said.

''Do you remember enough to play, or do you want me to show you a few moves?''

''Maybe you better show me a few moves,'' she said.

Deacon leaned his cue against the table and moved behind her. Her positioned his arms over hers and spoke directly into her ear.

''First make a bridge with your fingers,'' he said, moving her hands on the green velvet tabletop until they were adjusted to his satisfaction. Normally she used her knuckles to rest the cue on, but Deacon made her form a bridge.

When he pulled the cue back to start the break, she shifted her hips and deliberately rubbed her butt against his groin. She felt a shudder of awareness run through him, and the cue bounced on the table when he dropped it.

She glanced over her shoulder. ''You okay?''

"Fine. Do you have the idea?" He stepped away from her and picked up his cue.

"Yes," she said, taking her cue and breaking the balls.

"I can see you *have* played this game before," he said when she neatly sunk a striped ball.

"Maybe once or twice. But never for these odds. I'll take your pants now."

He removed his belt slowly and set it on the table while he bent down and removed his shoes and socks. Then he unfastened his pants and slid them down his legs. The hem of his shirt hung to the top of thighs, but when he tossed her his pants, she realized he wasn't wearing any underpants. She'd sadly underestimated her foe. And missed her next shot.

"I'll take your dress," he said. Leaning over the table, he sank his solid colored ball and turned to her, waiting to collect his prize.

Deacon had never suspected Kylie was capable of conning him. He liked it. He liked that there was more to her than he'd first glimpsed in the security camera. He liked that she'd went immediately for his pants, too. Because he didn't know how much longer he could let this game continue.

"Do I have to take the dress off entirely?" she asked, tipping her head to the side.

In a teasing mood, Kylie was more than he'd expected. Something had happened on the walk from the elevator to his suite. Something that had given her a confidence he'd known she had. Something that was responsible for the tingling in his veins. "I gave you my pants."

She moved to his side of the table, leaning nonchalantly next to him. He could smell those damned flowers again and something more elemental. The scent of a woman.

"Indeed you did. Say I unbuttoned the dress and left it hanging open, would that be enough?"

He ran his finger down the side of her neck, dipping it into the scooped bodice of her dress and caressing the upper curves of her breasts. He'd tasted her, knew the texture of her nipple in his mouth, but he didn't know its color. And he wanted to.

He wanted to carry her over to the patch of sunlight in front of the glass wall and spread her out on the floor so that nothing was hidden to him. And then make love to her with the city in the background.

"Only if you're not wearing any panties," he said, enjoying himself too much.

She bit her lower lip as she reached out to cup his face in her hands. Her fingers were cold but felt good against his jaw. She leaned up and brushed her lips against his. "Sorry to disappoint you, but I am wearing panties. Women's undergarments must be cheaper than men's."

He cupped her head and took her mouth in a long drugging kiss, only pulling back when she was standing on tiptoe, her fingers digging into his shoulders. His erection stirred against the tails of his shirt. "Or one of us might not be as eager as the other one."

"Don't underestimate me, Deacon," she said. Then slid her hands down his back and under his loose shirt. Her nails raked his buttocks.

"After watching you play pool, I doubt I will again." He dropped his cue and folded her into his arms. Leaning into his body, she nestled the center of herself against his arousal. Bending, he nipped at her collarbone.

"Stop stalling, angel."

"If you insist."

Backing a few steps away from him, she slowly unbuttoned the dress, revealing the curves of her breasts cupped in an ice-blue bra of sheer fabric. Her nipples beaded against the fabric. She stopped unbuttoning when she reached her waist and shrugged out of the bodice. Then she let the garment fall to the floor to pool at her feet.

She still wore her modest heels, but otherwise her body was clad in only the matching panty and bra. He hardened more. He felt so full he thought he might not need to be inside her body to come.

He picked up his cue. Though he wanted to pick

her up and put her on the table. "Next I'll take your panties."

"Are you sure you don't want the bra?" she asked, cupping her breasts and rubbing her fingers over the distended nipples.

"I want it. Just not yet."

He closed his eyes, trying to banish Kylie from his mind for a minute. But it was hard. He wanted her. And this teasing game that he'd intended to ease them into lovemaking was more torture than fun.

He opened his eyes and found her watching him. He lifted her by the waist and put her on the table in front of him. Bending, he took her nipple in his mouth, sucking fiercely on it until he felt her hands in his hair. She molded them to his head and kept him close.

He slipped his hands over her back, releasing the clasp of her bra, and then used his teeth to peel the fabric away from the creamy curves of her breasts.

"I wanted to do this at the pool."

She trembled under his hands. She unbuttoned his shirt and pushed it off his shoulders. He stood before her totally naked. Aware of her eyes on him, he flexed his muscles and stood still until she'd looked her fill.

She reached between them and ran her hands over his chest. Lingering on his nipples, scraping her nails over them, she then followed the tapering line of hair down his stomach to his groin. She took him in her hand, caressing his length with both of her hands.

Reaching between his legs, she cupped him. His breath hissed in through his teeth. He couldn't wait much longer. ''Take off your panties.''

She nodded. He bent and took a condom out of his pants pocket and quickly donned it. ''I can't wait this time.''

''Good.'' She hopped back onto the side of the pool table, leaning back on her elbows. She spread her legs and tilted her head to the side.

She looked so tempting, lying there waiting for him. He put his hands on her thighs, holding her legs apart while he lowered his head and kissed her center. She moaned his name. And her hands were once again holding his head.

Reaching up, he plucked at her nipples with both hands. She was twisting under him, her center dewy and sweet with cream. Her hips lifted toward him, and he licked and nipped at her until she was on the verge of climax. One more taste pushed her over the edge. The sounds she made as she came echoed in the room.

He lifted his head and looked down at this woman who was going to be his for the rest of his life and slid into her. She was tight, and despite her wetness, he had to pause to let her adjust to his width before sliding all the way home. She wrapped her legs high around his waist and he slid even farther into her.

He lowered his mouth to her breast and put his hands under her hips, lifting her into each of his thrusts.

She tightened around him. Her hands roamed down his back. They were touching everywhere. He nibbled his way up to her neck and suckled at a pulse point. He kept his thrusting strong, growing in momentum until he heard that catch in the back of her throat that signaled her orgasm.

The base of his spine tingled and he knew that his was just a breath away. He lifted his head and watched her face as her climax broke over her. Then he gripped her hips and thrust into her one more time, emptying himself with a force that made his knees buckle.

Deacon lifted her in his arms and carried her into the bedroom. Kylie tried not to cling too tightly to his shoulders, but the impulse was there. She wanted to wrap herself around him and hold him to her forever.

It scared her, feeling this intensely about a man she'd just met. But at the same time it was new and exciting and more than she'd ever imagined she could feel. Especially for a man like Deacon, who didn't show her very much of himself.

''You okay?'' he asked, his voice gruff.

She lifted her gaze to his and took a deep breath.

Okay? She doubted she'd ever be okay again. But she nodded. "Yes."

He set her in the middle of his bed, which was covered in a dark blue duvet. The blinds were closed, keeping out the sun. The room was light but still had shadows—which Kylie found comfortable because she wanted to hide from Deacon. She didn't want him to know or even suspect that her feelings for him were deepening by the hour.

He was someone used to gambling and living life on the roll of a dice. She was the opposite. She was used to routine. Used to calm steady waters, not waves, through which to move through life.

He lay down next to her on the bed and pulled her into his arms. She curved herself around him. Resting one thigh on top of his and putting her head on his chest, right over his heart.

She could hear it beating, the sound steady and solid and very reassuring. His hands moved up and down her back, and she knew from the tenor of the embrace he meant for it to be comforting.

And it was. But it was also very arousing. She'd never made love during the day before. She'd never been with a man, who even though he had work to do, would stop and dedicate the day to her. And in essence that's what Deacon had done.

Her stomach growled indelicately.

Deacon chuckled and put his knuckles under her chin, tilting her head back until she met his gaze.

She saw a lightness there she seldom saw. And though she was embarrassed, she felt a little better.

"Ready for brunch?" he asked with a wicked arch of one brow. "Or perhaps I should say lunch, now."

"I...yes. Sorry. I'm used to eating an early lunch."

"Why?"

"Because at work we have to cover the phones, and I drew the first lunch break."

"Do you like that?" he asked, propping himself up on his elbow. His free hand rested on her stomach and he looked down at her in that intense way of his she was coming to realize meant he was processing everything about her.

"What's to like? It's part of working."

"I can go to lunch whenever I want," he said with an expansive gesture that encompassed her and the bedroom.

"I haven't seen you eat anything yet today," she said. She wasn't about to explain office politics to this man who owned a hotel/casino. It'd be nice if she was the senior person in her office and able to decide when she wanted to go to lunch, but she wasn't. And she was working to pay off her house, so sometimes she had to do things she didn't necessarily want to do.

"Who said lunch was all about food?" he said, caressing her from her neck to her waist with languid strokes of his broad hand. He came close to touching her breasts, but stopped just shy of them. At last, using a forefinger, he traced the flesh at the bottom of one breast.

An incredible sense of fullness, of voluptuousness filled her. She shifted her shoulders against the duvet and tried with such movement to direct him where she wanted his touch.

She glanced up and realized he'd said something and was waiting for a response. Something about lunch and food? She didn't really care. She wanted him to make love to her again.

"What did you say?" she asked. She traced one finger down the center of his chest, following the patterns in the hair there. She loved the strength of him, but also the differences between the two of them. The way he made her feel so soft and feminine, just by being in the same room with her.

"That lunch isn't necessarily all about food," he repeated as she tiptoed her fingers closer to his groin.

"Oh," was all she said. She sat up to better see his body. Pushing on his shoulder, she urged him onto his back. She didn't kid herself that she'd manipulated him to where she wanted him. Deacon had lain back because he wanted to. Whether because he was indulging her or because he craved more of her touch she didn't know.

She shifted to her knees and touched his entire

body this time, starting at the top of his dark hair and stroking every inch of his flesh. Then she followed the same path with her lips and tongue. She did this twice, avoiding his groin completely the first time, just trailing her fingers over his body. And then the second time Kylie let her breath caress him.

He'd hardened even more than before. She lowered her head to drop a kiss on the tip of his erection. He held himself tense under her mouth and the hands that rested on his thighs.

She glanced up his body, some of her curls dropping to caress his length. "Like this?"

"Hell, yes," he said.

She turned back to him and took him into her mouth. He moaned her name when she reached between his legs to cup him intimately. She continued to suck at him until his hips left the bed and his hands bracketed her head. Then he pulled her up the length of his body.

Using his hands on her thighs, he positioned her on top of him. The feel of his erection against her flesh was a pleasure in itself—but reminded her they were close to having unprotected sex.

"Condom?" she said.

His hands were on her breasts, plucking at her nipples. His erection was nudging closer and closer to her center. And she was tempted to say the hell with it.

"Nightstand. Top drawer," he said.

She scooted up his body and leaned over to open the drawer and remove the box. She felt his breath on her nipple seconds before his lips closed around it. She almost dropped the box of condoms when he started suckling her. But she ached deep inside and she wanted Deacon now.

She wanted to reaffirm the bonds they'd forged in his living room. She wanted to reaffirm the bonds that her heart had started to make around his. She wanted to reaffirm that this man was quickly becoming much more than a vacation fling.

He held her with one hand behind her shoulder blades and the other moving over her body, bringing every inch of her to tingling awareness.

He lifted his mouth from her. "Find them?"

"Yes."

He took the box from her hands, opened a packet and reached between their bodies to sheathe himself. He did it quickly and efficiently and then glanced up to find her watching him.

He said nothing, only arched one eyebrow at her in question.

She only shrugged. No way was she going to say anything about how every action he made fascinated her.

He grasped her hips and arranged her over him, but didn't move to penetrate her. She opened her eyes and found him watching her. Waiting.

"What are you waiting for?" she asked.

"You. Ride me, angel."

She balanced herself with her hands on his shoulders, then slowly lowered herself over him until he was fully inside her. She began to rock her hips. He sat up, wrapped his arms around her body and held her close, content to let her set the pace. And it wasn't long before they were both shaking with their orgasms and clinging tightly to each other.

Deacon rolled them to their sides and held her close in the aftermath. Kylie closed her eyes, hoping to hide the truth of her emotions from him, but really wishing she could hide from the truth in her heart.

Eight

The next four days went by too quickly for Deacon. He wasn't a man for wishing, but now he wished with all his heart that time would slow down. He knew that the end of Kylie's vacation was approaching and that soon she would return to her old life. He also knew that he didn't want this courtship to end. The courtship was the best of both worlds.

She'd refused to move into his suite, but denied him nothing of her body. If he wanted to make love to her, she welcomed him, but stubbornly refused to spend the entire night in his bed. And for some reason he wanted her there. It was all he thought about when they were apart. Mac had been by a couple of times to check on the status of their bet, and Deacon had smiled with confidence and said it was a piece of cake. But Kylie wasn't as easy to read or play as the roulette wheel or a hand of cards.

He broke out in a sweat every time he thought about asking her to marry him. Every time he imagined her answer. Every time he watched her walk away from him.

He pushed those thoughts aside as he waited for Kylie on the roof helipad. He'd promised her an aerial tour of the area, including the Red Rock Canyon and Hoover Dam.

The door to the hotel opened, and Kylie came out onto the helipad, followed by Mandetti. Mandetti had said he needed a break from studying the casino operation and had volunteered to escort Kylie to the wax museum earlier that day because Deacon had been unable to break away from work.

Mandetti wasn't like any gaming-commission officer Deacon had ever met before. He liked the older man. If his mom was in town, instead of on a cruise in Hawaii right now, Deacon would've introduced the two of them.

He crossed the tarmac and placed a lingering kiss on Kylie's lips. The woman was becoming more important to him by the hour. And the fact that she fit his idea of wife didn't seem to matter much.

He had a hard time remembering that he was trying to woo her with slow moves. His gut said to claim her. To lock her in his bedroom and make love to her until she couldn't move. Until she forgot everything she'd known before him. Until she was his completely and none of this damned doubt remained.

But that wasn't in the plans today. So he forced a lightness he was far from feeling into his voice. "How was the museum?" he asked.

Kylie tipped her head to the side and smiled. Her expression of joy struck an answering chord deep within him. He wanted to make her happy. He knew he couldn't. He'd tried for years to make his mom happy until finally one day when he was eight, she'd told him one of life's truths. Each person had to find his or her own happiness. He couldn't manufacture a happy ending for her, she had to make her own happy ending, she said.

"Awesome. They looked so real. Didn't they, Angelo?"

Angelo? He arched an eyebrow at the older man, who just gave him a hard stare. Deacon turned away to keep from laughing.

"Thanks so much for coming with me," she added.

"You're welcome, *amico*. I'll leave you two to your tour. I need to get back to work."

"Thanks, Mandetti," Deacon said, shaking the older man's hand. He cupped Kylie's elbow and led her toward the helicopter.

She was wearing a close-fitting black top, a pair of khaki pants and black sandals. There was nothing remotely sexy about the outfit, but it turned him on, anyway.

"Who'll be the pilot today?" she asked as they neared the chopper.

"I will."

"You can fly?"

"I can pilot a helicopter."

"I can't."

"I'm not surprised," he said.

"Why not? Am I not the adventurous type?"

"Oh, you're adventurous, all right," he said.

She smiled at him. That secret smile she used only when they were alone together.

"Wow. I have a million questions," she said with a laugh.

No surprise there, either. Kylie was curious about everything. She had a million questions about stuff that Deacon admitted he'd just taken for granted.

"Ask away," he said.

She stopped on the tarmac and pivoted to face him. The large sunglasses she wore covered her eyes. Raising her hands to his shoulders, she leaned up and kissed him.

He wrapped his arms around her waist and tugged her more fully against his body. He tilted his head and leisurely explored her mouth with his. She sighed.

He lifted his head long minutes later and gazed down at her.

"I missed you this morning," she said.

He resisted the urge to hug her closer and never let go. To make promises he knew wouldn't hold up in the real world.

Damn. He was forgetting the rules he'd learned long ago. Forgetting the reasons he'd picked her out on the security camera. Forgetting she was here with him because he'd made a bet that he could convince her to marry him.

He didn't say anything, just urged her to the helicopter and opened the passenger door. "Put the earphones on."

She watched him with wounded eyes. He knew he hadn't reacted the way he should have. He knew he'd just lost some ground. But he had come too close to losing his focus. To forgetting the golden rule. Love was an illusion, and only a man looking for a fall forgot they were playing a game.

Deacon was a skilled pilot, which didn't surprise Kylie. He was good at everything he did. Especially kissing. She freely admitted she was addicted to his embrace. The only reason she hadn't stayed the night in his room was the very real fear that she'd start believing her vacation affair had turned into something else.

She said nothing as they took off, feeling a little

foolish for having said she missed him when clearly he didn't feel the same way. Deacon seemed to sense her awkwardness and filled the silence in the cockpit with a running monologue that sounded as though it came straight from a Nevada tourism guidebook.

She enjoyed hearing his observations, with which he peppered the tour-guide spiel. They gave her a chance to pretend he hadn't rebuked her earlier. A chance to put her ill-timed words behind them and pretend he'd forgotten she'd said them.

She knew he wasn't trying to hurt her. She knew she was the only one who could keep her heart intact. And she knew that the only way to do that was to remember that love, like fortune, could change on a roll of the dice. Only the savviest gambler should contemplated letting their heart ride on the outcome.

She took a deep breath and pushed aside her feelings. Deacon was funny, with a wry self-deprecating wit.

"My mom lives in Henderson. That's the city we're approaching now."

She glanced down. The small city was very different from the air than Vegas. "Are there casinos there?"

He banked to the left, taking them around the outskirts of town. "Nah. It's an industrial town."

"Did you ever live there with her?" she asked. Deacon talked so little about his personal life that she still felt as if she didn't really know him. But what did it matter? she asked herself. She was leaving tomorrow.

"No," he said.

"Why not?" Something in his voice touched her deep. And she knew she wasn't going to leave Vegas and the Golden Dream without leaving a little piece of herself behind.

"Because I want the good life," he said in that wry way of his that made her feel as if she should know more than she did.

"And do you have it?"

"A lot more than I did when Mom and I went our separate ways. But at least then, I had freedom and a chance to make it big."

"Obviously you made the most of that chance."

"Not even close," he muttered.

"Deacon?"

"Nothing, angel. Leave it alone."

Feeling put in her place once again, she stared out the window. Maybe he knew she was scheduled to go home tomorrow and wanted to remind her that their relationship would be ending. Maybe he—

He reached over, pushed the mike away from her mouth and cupped the back of her head. Leaning over, he kissed her hard and fast.

She stared at him. "What was that for?"

"For not having the words you might want to hear from me."

"I'm not looking for the words, Deacon. I had them once and they weren't sincere."

He said nothing and she realized that his silences meant more than she'd previously thought. She wasn't building castles in the air. She was building hopes around the fact that this man with the shattered soul would take a chance on an ordinary girl.

She watched the landscape rolling underneath them. Soon they were approaching another city. "What's that?"

"Boulder City," he said. "The only city in Nevada without legalized gambling."

"Are you scandalized?"

"Yeah, but not about that," he said. "The city was constructed while they were building the Hoover Dam."

"Why'd you learn to fly?" she asked as he banked the chopper and flew it directly over the historical district of Boulder City.

"One of my first jobs in Las Vegas was working at a tourist attraction on the strip that offered aerial tours. The guys who were pilots made more than us regular stiffs, so I started taking lessons."

"Do you always get what you want?" she asked. His willpower and self-control was amazing. There were a number of things she wanted—slim thighs, a nice car, a man who'd love her for her. But she'd never been willing to work up a sweat or to bypass something for her home or a fancy car. And she'd never been able to risk her emotions on man.

Not even Jeff, her ex-husband, had been worth the chance. A big part of her was afraid that like the other fairy tales that had disappeared with childhood, the myth of forever love was going to prove elusive.

"Kylie?"

"What?"

"I asked if you wanted to tour Hoover Dam. I made arrangements to land at a heliport near here."

"I'd love to. I've never been."

He nodded and concentrated on landing the chopper. She watched him and tried to determine if this was an elaborate scheme that Deacon had done more than once. Was this the way he treated all the women he was interested in? Was this part of a smooth operation to seduce a willing woman? Or was this something more?

She was afraid to believe it could be more. She scarcely knew the man. He was worlds different from her. He was used to having someone do everything for him. She was used to working in her garden and cleaning her house when things got too stressful outside her cozy little bungalow.

He landed the helicopter and came around to take her hand. Leading her to the waiting limo, she realized that they had more in common than either of them had wanted to acknowledge, because his hand around hers was tight and she sensed he had no plans to let her go. Or maybe that was just the hope of her foolish heart.

Deacon had planned every detail of this day, but his job kept getting in the way. They'd arrived back at the hotel nearly an hour ago and he'd planned a romantic dinner with Kylie, but instead, he was sitting in his office with Mandetti and two men from the gaming commission discussing Mandetti's findings.

Though the commission was happy with his work and wanted to use his hotel as a model of efficiency, Deacon wasn't really paying attention. He knew that when things were settled with Kylie, this good news would mean more. But tonight, knowing she planned to leave tomorrow, he needed to focus on her. He'd never asked anyone to marry him before. In the past the appeal of contemplating his relationship with a woman would have paled in comparison to hearing good news about his casino. But he'd come to realize that without the right woman by his side, business success wasn't as rewarding.

Finally the meeting ended and the men left—except Mandetti.

"Good job, *compare*."

"Thanks, Mandetti. I'm happy with the results. My offer's still open. Feel free to stay and enjoy the hotel for a few days."

"I'm taking you up on it. It's been a long time since I played in Vegas."

"I'll have my secretary take care of the arrangements."

Deacon left Mandetti with Martha and hurried to meet Kylie in the lobby. She was sitting where she'd been the first time he'd approached her. She was wearing her glasses and had a book in her hand, but was talking to a pretty redhead seated to her right.

Deacon slowed his steps and went over everything in his head one more time. He patted his pocket and felt the small jeweler's pouch he'd put there earlier. He'd intended to ask her to marry him at the top of Hoover Dam. But it hadn't felt right.

He'd been afraid her answer would have been no then. He realized that Kylie needed some things he'd never intended to give his wife. Words that were foreign to him. When she'd said earlier that she'd missed him, he'd felt more than a moment's fear. He'd felt panic. This wasn't familiar territory. And he knew enough about Kylie to know that she needed to show her affection for him, but also receive something in return.

That had been what stopped him. He had little to give any woman, apart from material things. Certainly Kylie had liked his expensive rooms, his big toys and playing in the casinos with his money, but she'd be just as happy with nothing. Deacon knew he had nothing beyond his little kingdom to offer her.

"Deacon," Kylie said, glancing up at him. She smiled that sweet half smile that made him want to be better than he was.

He walked toward her. She and the redhead stood up. He slipped his arm around Kylie's waist and dropped a quick kiss on her lips.

"This is Tina Sturgel, my friend and roommate. Tina, this is Deacon Prescott."

He took Tina's hand and dropped a kiss on the back of it. "It's a pleasure to meet you."

"Same. I've heard so much about you."

"All good," Kylie said with a laugh.

"Likewise," Deacon said.

"I'm heading up to the room. You two have fun tonight."

Tina disappeared and Kylie sidestepped out of his embrace. She took off her glasses, tucking them in her purse. "What are we doing for dinner?"

"Something special. But first you need a new dress and some pampering."

"Who says?" she asked with a gleam in her eye.

"I do. I want everything to be perfect tonight."

"Because it's my last night here?"

"Yes," he said.

"I was thinking about that," she said. She didn't look at him now, instead toyed with the strap of her handbag and glanced at the tourists walking through the lobby.

He waited. If she said she never wanted to see him again, he'd have to change his plans. Take her up to his living quarters and make love to her all night. Save the marriage proposal for the morning. When they were in bed she was curled up against him trustingly.

"I... Do you ever get to California?" she asked. Her voice was soft, her words tentative.

"No. Why?"

"I was going to invite you to stay with me and maybe show you around my town," she said.

Touched in a way he'd never been before, Deacon reached out and cupped her face, tilting her head back until her gaze met his. Leaning down, he kissed her as if she was the most precious woman he'd ever known. And the truth was—she was. "I'd love to come and stay with you."

She tilted her head to the side and watched him with eyes that made him feel ten feet tall. "So this doesn't have to end tomorrow?"

"No. In fact, I'd like for it to last a very long time."

"You don't seem like a long-distance-affair kind of guy."

"We can discuss that at dinner. Come. Let's get you a suitable dress," he said, dropping his hands to his sides.

"Where are we going?"

"To an exclusive boutique."

"Here?"

He nodded, leading her down a hallway. She slipped her arm through his and he took comfort from the feel of her pressed close to his side. There was something reassuring about holding her. One of the bellmen caught his eye and smiled as they walked by. And Deacon felt as if everything in his world was finally coming together.

Nine

Kylie was alone in the dressing room. She looked like someone she didn't recognize. The dress was a slim-fitting sheath overlaid with a light filmy material. She turned around in the mirror and looked at herself from all angles. She looked good, but not like herself.

The deep V in the front revealed her cleavage. She'd never imagined she could look like this. She swept her hair up with her hands and studied her reflection. The cut of the dress made her neck seem almost swanlike.

She bit her lip. She knew that most of her issues with wearing something like this stemmed from the fact that she was the plain sister. The one everyone expected to stay plain. But that didn't bother her. She liked knowing where she fit into the scheme of things. This dress smudged the lines of that nice neat picture she had planned of her life, and Kylie didn't know if she was ready to see herself in this new light.

"How's it fit?" Deacon asked.

Deacon in a woman's dressing room was like a tiger in a cage. He'd prowled restlessly from one end of the room to the other while she'd been trying on clothes.

"Fine. I don't think this one is going to work, either," she said. As tempted as she might be to actually buy the dress, she knew she'd be uncomfortable wearing it outside the dressing room.

"None of them work? I can't believe this. I'm going to get the owner."

"No, Deacon. Don't do that."

He sighed. His cell phone had rung several times while she was trying on clothes. He probably had better places to be than in a dressing room waiting for her to pick out a dress. "We'll go to the Chimera. I bet we'll find a dress there."

She sighed. He was being so nice. But this wasn't working. She was leaving for home in the morning and she didn't want to spend her last night with Deacon in the dressing room. "I don't want to go to another boutique."

"What's the matter, angel?"

She leaned her forehead on the dressing-room door. The tips of his Italian leather loafers were visible under the door. "Don't make me say it."

"Let me come in," he said gruffly.

She turned the handle and stepped back. He closed the door and leaned against it. Arms crossed over his chest, he studied her the way an art connoisseur would study a painting by one of the Dutch masters. "You look lovely."

Of course she did. When the price tag on a dress was just shy of a thousand dollars, one thing you could count on was a dress that fit well. "It's not me."

"Of course it is. This exactly what I had in mind for this evening." Gently he held her arms out from her sides. There was something innately sexual in his gaze now. She felt awareness spread through her body. Only Deacon had this kind of power over her.

He put his hand on her hip and turned her toward the mirror. He stood a few paces behind her in his designer suit. Seeing the two of them together in the mirror made her realize that they looked like a couple. A very good-looking and successful couple. Her lightness complemented his darkness.

"We look perfect," he said, sliding an arm around her waist and pulling her back to rest against him.

"Deacon, this isn't the real me."

He lowered his head to nibble on her neck. Shivers spread down her body, pooling in her center.

"I'd say this *is* the real you," he murmured against her skin.

She couldn't concentrate on how right it felt to be in his arms. She knew he didn't mean that the real her was the one in his arms. He meant the woman in the dress. "I'd never spend this much on one dress. Why can't I look at the sale rack? I'll find something there, I promise."

He shook his head. The hand on her waist started to move upward. Tracing the delicate pattern on the filmy over-dress.

"You don't have to buy off the sale rack. This is my gift to you."

"Well, I won't be able to eat in this gift."

"Why not? Is it too tight?"

The indulgent tone in his voice usually thrilled her, but today it sounded almost patronizing. "No, it's not too tight. I'd be worried about ruining it."

"I want to give you something nice. If not this dress, how about one of these?" he said, gesturing at the pile of rainbow-colored dresses the saleswoman had gathered for her at Deacon's request.

"It's not this dress. It's this place. I feel like…"

"Like what?" he asked, stepping away from her.

God, she missed his touch. How was she ever going to settle back into her old routine once she was home?

"An impostor. A fraud. Like I'm trying to be someone I'm not."

"You'd never do that, Kylie. Of all the people I've ever met, you are one of the few who really knows who she is."

"Yes, I do. But you don't know who I am."

He ran his fingers through his thick hair, sighing heavily. "I just want this to be a night to remember. I don't expect you to wear the dress every day."

"I'm making too much of this, aren't I."

"Yes. Why?"

"I...I gave up part of myself for my husband. I tried to be what he wanted in a wife and I vowed to never do that again."

"I'm not asking you to be an evening-gown-wearing woman."

"I know that in my rational mind. But my heart, Deacon, my heart is urging me to do whatever I have to in order to please you."

"You do please me, Kylie, in ways you'll never understand."

Deacon left the dressing room and paid for Kylie's dress and shoes. He asked the saleswoman, Maria, to send Kylie next door for a hair and makeup appointment. He left a note for Kylie explaining he'd return to take her to dinner.

He had some last-minute arrangements to take care of. Though Mac had ribbed him about it, Deacon had purchased one of those bridal magazines. He had found an article featuring the most romantic proposals and had decided to combine a few of them when he asked Kylie to marry him.

He wanted her to be so bowled over by him that she forgot his earlier faux pas. When he couldn't tell her how he felt. Admitting he'd missed her carried a price that was too high. That she forgot that sometimes, emotionally, he couldn't give her what she needed. That she forgot that maybe he wasn't the kind of guy she wanted forever.

He took his private elevator to his penthouse apartment. As ordered, there was a candle on every surface. He had his Bose CD player keyed up for a compilation of Ella Fitzgerald and Miles Davis songs. He hoped the music would be a pleasant reminder for her of their first date.

There were two large vases filled with roses—six dozen in all. A discreet jewelry box containing a stunning diamond choker and matching bracelet sat on a table. Rose petals were strewn on the floor leading to the bedroom.

Everything was perfect. So why was he sweating? This was just what the magazine said every woman wanted. He had planned every detail to guarantee success. But if he knew anything about Kylie, it was that she was unpredictable.

His cell phone rang. "Prescott."

"Hey, buddy, tonight's the big night, right?" Mac

had been keeping track of his courtship of Kylie. Utilizing the many security cameras that lined the strip it had been shockingly easy for Mac to spy on them. In fact, it was virtually impossible to have any real privacy in Las Vegas.

"Don't you have a hotel to run?" Deacon asked.

"I can do that in my sleep. Watching you plan the perfect proposal is definitely more interesting."

"Back off, Mac."

"Hey, I was only kidding. She's going to say yes. And I'm not even going to mind losing the bet."

"Goodbye, Mac."

"Good luck, Deacon."

Mac hung up and Deacon straightened his tie one last time. He patted his pocket for the ring. He'd ordered it from a jeweler that Mac had recommended in New York City and had had it flown in by special courier.

He checked on the bottle of champagne that was chilling, called the kitchen to make sure everything was as he'd ordered for dinner and then had no choice but to cool his heels while he waited to go meet Kylie.

He paced to the window and looked out at the city. His city. Vegas embodied everything that was Deacon: past, present and future. Kylie was the key to moving from casino-owner upstart to upper-class society. She would give credibility to everything he'd worked so hard to accomplish.

He checked his watch and went back downstairs to meet Kylie. He met the photographer he'd hired to take pictures of the two of them. Josh was a new employee to the Golden Dream but had earned his reputation in Los Angeles by photographing celebrities. Deacon had paid top dollar for Josh tonight because he'd learned the hard way that you get what you pay for.

And if you'd never really had anything, then you had to pay a little more for everything.

"We'll meet you by the El Dorado. I'm going to have the security guys trigger the waterfall when we're ready for the picture."

"You're the boss."

Deacon nodded and walked away. He took a deep breath and reassured himself that he had nothing to lose this evening. If Kylie said no… She wasn't going to say no. He'd bet good money on it. A lot more than good money.

The door to the salon opened as he approached and Kylie entered the hallway. For a minute he couldn't speak. He could just stare at her. She was everything he'd imagined she'd be and more. Her hair was piled on top of her head with a few tendrils framing her face. Her eyes were wide and serious as she met his gaze, and he felt his heart beat speed up.

He wanted to toss her over his shoulder and carry her back to his cave. He wanted to mark her as his and make sure that no one, not even Kylie, especially not Kylie, ever forgot she was his.

"What do you think?"

"Beautiful, angel. You're beautiful."

"I'm kind of amazed," she said, walking slowly toward him.

She stopped only inches from him, resting her hands on his shoulders, the way she always did before she leaned up to kiss him. But she didn't lean up. She just stood there watching him. Studying him and searching, he imagined, for some answer in his expression to a question only she knew.

"I realized I'd been remiss earlier in the dressing room," she said at last.

"Remiss?" he asked. God, he couldn't think when she ran her tongue over her lower lip. Everything masculine in him was on red alert. He was a heat-seeking missile and he knew the target was in sight. He inclined his head and settled his hands on her waist.

She had about thirty seconds to say whatever it was she wanted to say before he was going to claim the kiss they both needed.

"Yes, remiss," she said. She bracketed his face with her hands and pulled his head a little closer to hers. Rising on tiptoe, she smiled at him and brought her lips to his.

"Thank you," she said against his mouth.

He showed his appreciation for her gratitude with

a kiss that left nothing to doubt. He tried to show her with his embrace all the things he'd never been able to say to her out loud. Because as she'd walked toward him, he'd realized why this one woman was making him sweat.

It didn't matter the cost; he'd gladly pay double just as long as he could be guaranteed she'd stay in his arms and in his life forever. And for the first time ever, he offered a silent prayer, wishing for the luck he'd always taken for granted to hold true.

She was aware that Deacon took complete control of the embrace, his mouth moving over hers with a surety that brought every nerve ending to life. Her breasts felt full and aching, needing more than just contact with his chest. She slipped her hands down his chest, caressing him. His hands on her back shifted, sliding down to cup her buttocks and lift her more fully against him. She shuddered at the full-body impact.

She knew he worked out twice a day. He'd brought her with him to the gym once and then took her to the jogging track on the seventeenth floor twice. But Kylie wasn't a big fan of exercise, so she'd ended up just watching him.

He worked hard for the muscles she loved to feel under her.

This made the ordeal of shopping for a dress and becoming someone she didn't recognize worthwhile.

There was a genuineness in Deacon's embrace that confirmed what she'd started to feel for him. Confirmed that her heart and her mind were on the same page, because Deacon had proved himself to be much more than a vacation lothario.

Kylie had felt like Cinderella getting ready for the ball. But she remembered what happened to some princesses and knew that sometimes fairy tales didn't work out.

Suddenly he dropped his arms and pulled away from her. "Dammit."

Concerned, she watched him as he paced to the wall and muttered another curse.

"You okay?" she asked. The man she'd come to know never lost his cool. And he also never stopped any physical embrace between them until they'd both been fully satisfied. She was still aroused, still aching and still very much in need of Deacon.

"Yes," he replied. "But I almost forgot my plans for this evening."

He shoved his hands in his pockets as she moved closer to him.

"I'd say a change in plans is in order," she said, wetting her lips.

"Stay there. Everything has to be perfect."

Now he was confusing her. Deacon had shown himself to be flexible. What kind of plans did he have for tonight that he was afraid to break? "Why?"

"I want this to be a night to remember."

"Every night with you is a night to remember," she said. Deacon had changed the way she looked at men and relationships. He'd changed her in so many ways. There wasn't another man who'd have gone the distance he had to make her feel this… precious to him.

He gave her a half grin, for the first time tonight looking like the man she'd come to know. "We aim to please."

"And you do," she said.

"Come on. The evening awaits."

He put his hand under her elbow and led her back through the hotel and outside. "Where are we going?"

"To the El Dorado. I've hired a photographer to take some pictures of us."

A nervous knot formed in the pit of her stomach. Why had Deacon gone to so much trouble for this night? The only answer she could come up with was one that made her hands shake.

The photographer posed her and Deacon in front of the waterfall. And then Deacon radioed someone and the waterfall turned to gold. Her job was just to look up at Deacon. And that was easy to do. His cold gray eyes were filled with a warmth she'd never seen in them before. She knew her own eyes were filled with love—and clearly broadcasting that emotion.

Deacon brought one hand up to her face and lowered his head to kiss her softly. Then he pulled back and she felt a certain magic at being here in this time and place with this man.

Everything else disappeared and she focused solely on Deacon. On the man who'd become the center of her world. She stifled her fear of loving a man who lived in a world that was totally foreign to her. In a world she'd had fun visiting, but could never be comfortable in.

"Perfect," Josh said.

His voice startled her. Deacon was such a dominant personality that he made everything else disappear. She'd forgotten that they weren't alone.

"Now I want one where you're both looking at me," the photographer said.

Deacon kept his arms around her as they turned. Josh snapped a few more pictures, telling them to tilt their heads this way or that. Then he paused to reload the digital memory card in his camera.

"This'll take a minute."

Deacon thrust his hands into his pants pockets before nodding at the photographer. "Come sit down with me, Kylie."

"Why?" she asked. He was nervous and a part of her wanted to needle him about it. Everything in his behavior was different tonight.

"Because I asked you to."

She had to bite her lip to keep from smiling. Deacon was so used to being in charge, she thought.

He led her to a wrought-iron bench near a small fountain and seated her on it. ''I have something to ask you.''

''Okay.''

''Will you marry me?''

Ten

Deacon waited for her answer. Time stood still and he heard the sounds of a couple arguing near the pool. Heard the rustling of leaves behind the bench and heard his own racing heartbeat in his ears.

He pulled the ring from his pocket and removed it from the velvet bag. Still Kylie said nothing. She watched him with eyes that were unreadable. He'd never been more aware of the unpredictability of women. Or the fact that he'd never understood them.

He took the ring from the bag. She gasped when she saw it. A flush spread over her face and neck, and he wished he'd done this in the privacy of his suite, so he could have made love to her first. Who knew if those bride magazines were right? Wouldn't Kylie have enjoyed a proposal in bed after they'd both made love?

But it was too late now. The hand had been dealt and had to be played out. He dropped down on one knee. Something he sensed Kylie would find romantic. All he needed was to hear one word from her lips, and this entire backdrop of romance would be worthwhile.

He heard Josh moving around behind him. God, if this didn't work out right, he was going to look like a fool. But then the biggest risks in a casino always yielded the biggest payoffs.

And Kylie was a huge payoff. The one thing he couldn't control or make happen on his own. A part of him—the little boy who'd always craved acceptance—held his breath. But the man he'd become was realistic and knew that there were more women in the world. Still, there was a sense of rightness about the two of them that made the thought of asking another woman to marry him seem impossible.

She was worth more than he'd ever have guessed when he'd first glimpsed her in the security monitor. She was more than that faceless Ralph Lauren model holding a child. When he looked at Kylie now, he could easily see her holding a little girl with her eyes and his dark coloring. He saw the seeds of the future in her, and he'd never experienced that in a person before.

"Oh, Deacon," she said, reaching tentatively for the ring. He took her hand in his. Her fingers were cold. Realizing she was nervous, too, comforted him.

He brought her hand to his mouth and kissed the back of it. He felt the shiver that went through her. After slipping the ring onto her finger, he admired his mark on her.

He liked having marked her. He liked the idea that any man who came near Kylie would automatically be aware that she belonged to him. And that she would be felt right in his soul.

Not because of any wager he'd made with Mac. Not because he didn't want to lose face in front of Josh or Mandetti or the staff members at the Golden Dream who knew he'd asked her to marry him. But because life with Kylie would be brighter than he'd ever imagined.

"Is that a yes?"

She took a breath, watching him with those wide eyes of hers. "Is this why you wanted everything to be perfect?"

He nodded. He was afraid to open his mouth again, knowing he'd demand an answer from her. He was in agony waiting to know if she was going to say yes.

"Oh, Deacon. This is…magical. Yes, I'll marry you."

He stood and pulled her to her feet, then leaned

down to take the kiss he needed. He was fairly certain dinner was going to have to wait. He needed to get her back to his suite and make love to her. To reaffirm the bond they'd forged over the past few days. To strengthen the bond they'd been building on. To make unbreakable the bond he knew would be the most important one in his life.

"I got the proposal," Josh said. "Nice touch down on one knee."

Deacon pulled back from Kylie and looked at the man. He didn't give a damn what that bridal magazine said—they had enough photos for this evening. "Thanks, Josh. That's all we need tonight. I'll contact you in the morning about wedding photos."

Josh turned and walked away, leaving Deacon alone with Kylie. "Let's go celebrate."

The magic of the evening didn't end. Deacon escorted her up to his rooms which looked like every woman's dream of a romantic setting, Kylie thought. Candles blazed on every surface and roses were everywhere, their scent filling the room. Deacon lifted her in his arms to carry her over the threshold.

He put her down quickly and stepped away. But not before she'd felt his erection against her side. The fact that he was taking such pains not to let their physical relationship overshadow the romance of the evening touched her, and she decided that tonight she'd reward him by giving him whatever he wanted from her.

He pulled out a chair at the dining table and seated her. Miles Davis trumpet riffs filled the room, and she felt the warm desert breeze, just as she had the first night they'd been together.

He'd gone to great lengths to make this night special for her, and she couldn't help but fall a little more deeply in love with him.

"Thanks for doing all this for me," she said.

"You're welcome. I've never asked a woman to marry me before and don't plan to ever again, so I figured I should make it a night to remember."

"You have. I can't believe you asked me to marry you."

"Having second thoughts already?" he asked, pouring champagne into two flutes.

"No. It's just so incredible. I've got to call my parents and let them know."

"Want to call them now?"

"No. They're in France, in wine country. I'm not sure of the exact time there, but I think it's the middle of the night."

"Do you want to wait for them to return before we wed?"

"I hadn't thought about it. When do you want to get married?" she asked.

"Tomorrow. I thought we'd do it before your friends leave. But I'd forgotten about your family."

Tomorrow. Wow, that was fast. She closed her eyes for a minute to block out all the trappings and really focus on what she wanted. Was marrying Deacon the right thing? Her heart said yes, but her mind said he was moving way too fast.

Yet at the same time, getting married with her friends present tomorrow seemed a perfect ending to her vacation. "I think I'd like that. I can wear this dress."

"No. You have to have a wedding gown. I've arranged for a fitting here in the morning."

She didn't want to go through a fitting. Dressing up tonight was enough for her. And she especially didn't want to wear a white gown. She'd had enough of the production that most weddings turned into her first time down the aisle. Of course, with her parents absent, it would be simpler. The last time her groom had been in full military dress and her brothers-in-law, as well.

"I was married before, so I don't want a big white gown."

"What do you want?" he asked, reaching across the table, taking her hand in his. She felt like the center of Deacon's world when he looked at her that way.

What she really wanted was just him. But she doubted he'd understand what she meant. She wanted something quiet and intimate. She'd had the big show the first time and had realized that having the perfect wedding didn't mean a perfect marriage. Or even a happy one.

"We have a lot to discuss," she said.

"Yes, we do. I hope you'll understand that I can't move to California. Will living here suit you? You can redecorate this place or we can build a house."

God, her job. She'd have to give notice and find another job. Some of the magic of the evening was waning. "Let's wait and talk about it tomorrow."

Deacon nodded. "I'll take care of everything."

The music changed and Ella Fitzgerald come on, singing "The Memory of You." Deacon stood and held his hand out to her. She let him help her to her feet and he pulled her into his arms. Deacon was a good dancer and they fit well together.

She rested her head on his shoulder as they swayed in time to the music. He pressed his lips to her temple and murmured words too soft for her to understand.

"What?" She lifted her head to look at him.

"You've made me a very happy man tonight," he said, then turned away. She knew displays of emotion didn't come easily to Deacon, and felt in that moment that he must feel the same way she did. That together they shared a depth of feeling that was found only once in a lifetime.

He radioed the restaurant and asked for dinner to be served. In no time, a trolley was wheeled into the dining area and dishes set on the table. Deacon said nothing until the staff had left and they were once again alone.

"I had a hot dinner prepared so I wouldn't be tempted to skip the meal."

"I wouldn't have minded eating a cold supper," she said. She liked that she could make Deacon forget about business or his plans. There was a heady sense of power and knowledge of her femininity that came with that.

"I would. There's more to us than just what we have in bed."

"I know."

"Sometimes it's easy for me to forget it."

"I'll remind you."

And she would. That was her job as his wife. And this time she was going into the marriage with her eyes open. She had no unrealistic sitcom-family illusions of what marriage should be, and she knew that Deacon had taken the time to know the real her. That he was marrying the woman she was with no expectations that she'd fill some role in his mind of what a wife should be.

Deacon waited until they'd finished dining before leading Kylie by the hand down the hall to the bedroom. "I've got something special planned for dessert."

More candles flickered in the bedroom. Rose petals littered the floor. And on the dresser was their last course—strawberries on ice and three different dipping sauces.

"Oh, Deacon. This is beautiful," she said. She let go of his hand and moved around the room. Taking off her shoes, she closed her eyes as she wriggled her toes in the rose petals.

"Ready for some payback?"

"Hell, yes, angel. But not yet. This night is for you."

She crossed back to him. Took his tie in her hand and pulled him across the room to the bed. Pushing gently, she forced him to sit on the bed. "This night is for *us*. And you've already given me enough."

"But I have one more gift for you."

"No more. Not now. I want to make love to my fiancé. I want to make this night special for you, too."

Her words made him feel good in a way he never had. His heart actually beat a little faster, and it had nothing to do with the knowledge that they were going to be having sex soon. Well, maybe a little to do with that. But a bigger part of him was stunned that this beautiful woman who was the key to his dreams felt so strongly about becoming his wife.

"You already have by saying you'd marry me."

She canted her head to the side. "Then let me show you how happy I am that you asked me to be your wife."

"Gladly, but with two conditions."

"The first?"

"That you wear only these two items." He took the diamond choker out of the box on the nightstand. She gasped when she saw it.

"Turn around."

She did and he fastened the choker around her neck. Unable to resist the smooth expanse of her neck, he lowered his head and bit her gently, then soothed the spot with his tongue and lips.

"Now give me your wrist," he said.

She did and he fastened the matching bracelet around her small wrist.

"Your second condition?" she asked breathlessly.

"That you let me return the favor of showing you how much your agreeing to be my wife pleases me. I think our dessert will keep."

"Agreed. Now, if you'll have a seat."

"Do you have a CD player in here?" she asked.

"Yes. What CD do you want to hear?" What kind of music would this sweet woman choose to dance to? Most nightclubs had hard-driving rock.

"I can get it. Something jazzy I think—you like jazz."

"I do." And I like you, he thought. Deacon seated himself on the bed. He kicked off his shoes and removed his belt before piling the pillows behind his back. Unless he missed his guess, he was about to be treated to a very special strip tease. For a minute he felt every jaded moment of his life weighing heavily on his shoulders. He'd been in strip clubs before he was fourteen.

Women and their bodies had never been a mystery to him, but with Kylie everything was new. Until Kylie, he'd never realized that seeing one woman could be special.

She flipped through the CDs in a case near the player. At last she made her choice and fiddled around with the volume and track selection. Soon the sounds of Steely Dan's "Babylon Sisters" filled the room.

It wasn't a song he'd have thought was seductive. But when Kylie turned to him and crossed the room with slow steps, her hips swaying to the beat, he thought it was the most seductive tune he'd ever heard.

His eyes tracked every movement she made. She ran her hands up and down her hips, sliding them over the soft fabric. With each stroke up her thighs, she lifted the hem of the dress higher, teasing him with more and more of the skin he was dying to see. Finally the tops of her lacy white garters were visible to him.

He was so aroused he had to spread his legs. He could actually feel his pulse in that part of his body. He wasn't sure if he could play this hand out. But the gleam in Kylie's eyes strengthened his resolve.

She unzipped her dress and let the bodice fall

away from her body. He was teased with glimpses of her flesh as she danced and shimmied closer to him. Gravity pulled the material lower with a slowness designed to keep him hanging on the precipice of anticipation.

Finally, as she reached the edge of the bed, the dress fell to her waist. She winked at him and shook her hips with the grace of a belly dancer. ''I took belly dancing last winter with my girlfriends. What do you think?''

The dress fell to the floor and she stood in front of him, wearing only her pretty bra and matching panties, a pair of thigh-high hose, the jewelry he'd given her and a pair of heels. She had legs that would do a showgirl proud.

''I'm not sure I can be objective,'' he said.

''Sure you can. Weren't you interviewing dancers for the new show today?''

''Yes,'' he said, reaching for the buttons on his shirt and slowly opening them. ''Do you want me to consider you for the show?''

Her eyes widened. ''I'm not…''

''Not what? Sexy enough? Bold enough?''

He knew she had some doubts about her sexuality but he'd have thought spending all that time in his bed would have erased most of them.

''You're right,'' she said, thrusting back her shoulders and tossing her hair. ''I am sexy and bold enough to be a showgirl. At least for you.''

He shrugged out of his shirt and tossed it aside. He sat on the edge of the bed and drew her closer to him. Her skin was hot and flushed from her exertions. He'd never had a woman affect him so deeply. He couldn't wait any longer to make love to her.

He tugged her forward until she rested between his spread legs.

"What are you doing?" she said. "I'm in charge."

"Not anymore." He grabbed her by the waist and tugged her down on top of him. Falling backward, he cushioned their fall to the bed.

He caressed his way up her spine, unfastened her bra and then pulled the fabric away from the globes of her breasts with his teeth. He took her nipple into his mouth and suckled. She rocked against him, her hands sweeping up and down his chest.

She pinched at his nipples and his hips jerked upward. He was on the edge. He desperately wanted to be inside her. But it was important that Kylie be with him tonight.

He slipped his hand inside her panties and tested her, finding her ready for him. He pushed her panties down her and she kicked them away.

"Move up on the pillows, Deacon."

He scooted back, unfastening his pants. Kylie helped him get rid of them and his boxers, as well. He reached for the condoms in the nightstand and sheathed himself.

Kylie moved up and he put his hands on her hips to help her position herself over him. Then she braced her hands on his shoulders and looked right in his eyes as she slowly lowered herself onto him.

She shuddered as he filled her. Her eyes drifted closed and her head fell back. Then she paused. Just held him there deep inside her while the walls of her vagina contracted around him. He tried to keep still but couldn't. She felt too tight, too good around him. He had to move.

Tightening his fingers on her hips, he lifted her off him and then thrust upward while he brought her back down. He did that two more times before he felt the telltale tingling at the back of his spine that signaled his pounding orgasm. Shifting up off the pillows, he took her nipple in his mouth again and suckled her hard until he heard the catch in the back of her throat that he'd learned signaled her approach to climax. He waited until she started to clench convulsively around him and then thrust one more time deeply inside her. He cradled her in his arms as they both returned to earth.

Their hearts beat in sync; and for the first time he had a feeling that he might actually get to a place in life where he was comfortable with himself and his world. And he knew that it was only with Kylie by his side that he could achieve that.

Eleven

Less than a week later, Kylie returned to Las Vegas on Deacon's private jet. He was in a meeting when she arrived at the hotel and she was at loose ends, no longer on vacation. She prowled restlessly through the casino, where she ran into Angelo Mandetti.

"What are you still doing here, Angelo?"

"I don't know. I thought my assignment was finished but I guess that just proves I'm still a *babbeo* sometimes."

"Have you seen Deacon?"

"Not this morning. I'm going up to the security room for a meeting with the head of that department.

Want to come with me? I'll show you how to use the surveillance cameras to locate your husband.''

Their wedding had taken place two days after Deacon's proposal. It had been small and intimate, and she'd found out quickly that her new husband delighted in indulging her. He'd arranged for her parents to fly back early from their trip and called both her sisters who'd flown in from the coast for the ceremony. The actual ceremony had taken place under a tent in the desert where they'd had their first date.

''You can do that?''

''Sure. That's how Deacon spotted you the first time. Didn't he tell you?''

''No. Will you?''

''*Madon'*. I guess so. He zoomed on you and decided you were the woman for him.''

Kylie wouldn't have guessed that Deacon was the love-at-first-sight kind of guy, but it fit with what he'd said about fate the first night they met.

''Thanks, Angelo. I'd love to see the security room. Maybe I can find Deacon and surprise him.''

Mandetti lead the way to the employees-only area and up a carpeted stairwell. Deacon kept promising her a tour of the casino, but so far he hadn't had the time and they'd gotten no farther than the roulette table. His job was very demanding. In fact, that was why she'd gone to Glendale by herself to pack up her house.

Deacon promised her a month-long vacation in Fiji once she returned. She was looking forward to time away with her new husband. She glanced down at the showy engagement ring and simple wedding band. A sense of love and satisfaction filled her. Even her father, who rarely showed any emotion, had told her how happy he was for her to have found a man like Deacon.

"Here we are," Angelo said, leading her into a dimly lit room filled with security monitors. A wall of glass separated them from the security guards who were on duty.

"What's this room for?"

"For Deacon's private use so he doesn't have to interrupt the security team."

"Good idea."

"That man of yours has made several innovative procedures here. That's why I'm still here. Documenting them so that we can propose several of them be added in other hotels."

Kylie didn't know what to say. She was proud of Deacon. She knew he'd worked hard to achieve everything he had and he must be very glad to know that others were recognizing his efforts. She knew that he had Vegas in his blood. It was only fair that he give back to the city that he claimed as his own.

Kylie walked to the bank of monitors and saw the shops, the pool, the casinos and the lobby. Angelo fiddled with some buttons on a keypad and the high-stakes rooms came up. Deacon was alone in one of the rooms with a man she didn't recognize.

"Who's that?"

"Hayden Mackenzie, owner of the Chimera hotel and casino."

"Is he a friend of Deacon's?"

Angelo nodded.

"Can we hear what they are saying?"

"Yes. Here's the volume key."

Kylie turned it up until Deacon's deep voice filled the room. She leaned closer to watch his face change as he talked. There was something inherently masculine in everything he did. But today he seemed more macho—which she knew sounded silly. Probably it was the way he was holding his shoulders. He seemed broader or taller.

"I never thought you'd go through with the wedding," Hayden said. "Was winning that important to you?"

"I told you from the beginning that she'd be my wife and she is. The rest is immaterial."

"I'm not so sure about that. But you won the bet."

"That's not your concern. I'll have the financial analyst from the children's shelter contact you."

"You do that."

Kylie turned away from the monitors. Angelo was still in the room with her and watching her carefully. "I'm sorry, *cara mia*."

"Why are you sorry? Oh, God, did you know about this bet, too?"

"Yes."

"What was the bet, Angelo? Tell me the details."

"It's not as bad as you think."

"I'll make up my own mind," Kylie said, wrapping her arms around her waist, then dropping them as she realized the gesture broadcast her vulnerability. "Why me?"

"I don't know all the details, only that he saw you on the monitor and said he was going to marry you. Mac offered him a wager. To meet and marry you within two weeks."

"I made it so easy for him," she said more to herself than to Mandetti.

"You're both happy now."

"Yes, we are. But how long will that last? Until Deacon has spent his winnings?"

"Kylie—"

"Thanks for the tour, Angelo."

She opened the door and walked down the long hallway. Her thoughts swirled around in her head. Maybe this was all a misunderstanding. Maybe there was a positive spin on this she was missing. But it didn't feel that way.

It seemed as if her dreams of happily-ever-after had once again been crushed. She'd given her heart once again to a man who didn't really want it.

She couldn't face him again. But she had nowhere

to go. She'd rented out her house in Glendale to a co-worker, and she didn't want to let anyone know that once again Kylie Smith had been a fool for love.

Deacon was feeling pretty good. His children's shelter was getting a new wing. The Golden Dream was going to be used as an example of innovation by the gaming commission. And most important, Kylie was coming home today.

He hadn't expected to miss her as much as he had. He left the high-stakes room and walked through the casino. He checked his watch and called Martha to find out if the jet had landed.

"She's been in the hotel for the last ninety minutes, sir."

"Why didn't you notify me?" he asked.

"You didn't ask me to," Martha said. She hung up before he could respond. He knew his secretary well enough to know that he'd just ticked her off.

He went to the private bank of elevators and waited impatiently for the car to arrive. He stuck his keycard in and leaned against the wall as the car carried him to Kylie.

He had a very intimate reunion planned for them. And when he had her naked in bed and totally sated, he wanted to talk to her about their honeymoon in Fiji. Mostly he just wanted to hold her and listen to the cadence of her breathing. To breathe in the scent of her and then fall asleep wrapped around her.

He opened the door to his suite and ran into Kylie coming out, with a suitcase in each hand. Her eyes were puffy and red. He pulled her into his arms, the suitcases slamming against his legs. What had happened? He rubbed his hands down her back trying to soothe her.

He'd never really been any woman's hero before, but being Kylie's felt right. He wanted to shelter her from harm and fight her battles. But Kylie wasn't looking at him as if he was her hero.

"Where are you going?" he asked carefully, maneuvering them back into his apartment.

"Home," she said. She moved a few paces away.

"This is your home now." Reminding them both of something he'd been so sure of just moments earlier.

"I thought, so too, Deacon, but now I'm not so sure."

"I can't argue with you if I don't have all the cards," he said. He'd noticed that about women. Sometimes they were angry about something only they knew, and guys were forced to try to sidestep the emotional mine fields and guess what they'd done wrong. It had happened before, but for some reason he'd never expected it to happen with Kylie.

"And you're such a big believer in making sure everyone knows all the details, right?"

He took her suitcases from her and walked into the living room. He put her luggage down next to him and leaned back against the pool table. Obviously he'd left out a detail at some time. When? "Tell me what's going on."

She pushed a strand of hair back behind her ear and watched him with those wide green eyes of hers. "It's so hard to decide where to start."

"At the beginning," he said.

She paced around the pool table to the bank of windows on the far side of the room. He saw her reflection in the glass. The woman looked aloof and alone. Not at all like his Kylie, a woman who exuded a quiet enthusiasm for everything she saw. Today it wasn't there.

"When I got back to the hotel today, I was wandering around looking for you and ran into Angelo in the casino. He offered to show me the security cameras so I could find you."

"And did you?" he asked. Damn. He'd been with Mac for the last forty-five minutes.

"Yes, I did. You were talking to Hayden MacKenzie about a wager—me."

He straightened and walked toward her. "Now, Kylie—"

She held up a hand to ward him off. He was reminded of how she'd used her book as a shield that first time he'd tried to talk to her. Her defense mechanisms were firmly back in place, it seemed.

"*Don't*. Don't try to explain it. I'm not ready to

hear anything from you right now. I just want to go away and pretend this never happened."

"But it did happen. And it's not the way you think. I had already decided to go after you before Mac proposed his wager."

She pivoted all the way around to face him. She blinked rapidly and he knew she was trying not to cry. He was a bastard. He'd always known it, but he'd fooled himself into believing that he'd left all that behind by carving out a better life for himself. It was humbling to realize how little he'd changed.

"You bet on me, Deacon. I can't get my mind around it."

"I bet on everything, angel. You know that. It was nothing."

"Why would you make a bet like that?"

"Mac knew I'd decided to find the right sort of wife, and he didn't think I could convince you to marry me."

"What's the right sort of wife?"

"You are."

"You didn't know me."

"You had the right look."

"I was wearing my glasses. I didn't look like a glamorous woman, the kind of woman you'd want."

"That's precisely why I *did* want you. You were quiet and refined. Everything I needed in a wife."

"You married me because I fit an image in your head?" she asked.

"Yes. The perfect wife."

"Dammit, Deacon. I'm not a cardboard cutout. I'm a real woman and I don't fit neatly into any role. I thought you knew me better than that."

"I do," he said, realizing the more he talked, the worse the conversation was going. He knew about luck and wagering and it was definitely time to fold his hand and retreat. There'd be another hand and another game. One he'd be better able to win when he was prepared for the game.

"What made me your idea of the perfect wife?" she asked.

Ah, hell. This wasn't going to end well. He knew it. He glanced at his cell phone, which for once was silent. "I…uh…"

"Stalling is not going to help. I want to know."

"Angel, it's not like that. I may have started out with an image of a perfect woman to fill the role of wife and hopefully someday mother, but once I got to know you, I realized you were the only woman for me."

"Really?"

"Yes, really." He closed the gap between them and swept her into his arms. This was much better. Shyly her arms came around his waist and she rested her head over his heart.

"I'm so glad to hear that. I'd thought you must feel the same way about me as I do about you."

"How do you feel about me, angel?"

"I love you," she said, looking up at him.

His stomach dropped and his feelings of security fled. He could handle anything but this. Anything but love. The one illusion he knew didn't really exist because he'd seen it change on the roll of the dice.

Kylie waited to hear Deacon return her words. To hear that he loved her, too. But he said nothing. His hands froze on her back, and she knew she'd misjudged him again. Whatever he may when he'd said he'd married her for who she was, she realized he hadn't married her for love.

Her heart broke all over again. And she stepped away from him, afraid to look at him or she'd start crying. God, this wasn't what she'd expected when she married Deacon.

"You don't love me, do you, Deacon," she said. Did she really sound that needy? Her voice was husky.

Deacon ran a hand through his hair and then tipped his head to the side. "What is love but the ultimate illusion?"

"Love isn't an illusion." Love was the one thing she'd always believed in. One thing she'd searched for time and again. It was an emotion she believed in and had seen concrete proof that it existed in her parents' marriage.

"To you, maybe, but here in Vegas it is an illusion. Some men think the dice love them. That Lady

Luck loves them. That the woman they met in the bar loves them. But once you leave Vegas, that love disappears.''

She tried to cut him some slack. If she'd grown up surrounded as he had, by gamblers, showgirls and the like, she might have a similar outlook on love. But she'd given Deacon her heart and he was saying her love was an illusion. ''I'm not like those other people,'' she said. ''I'm not fickle. I know my mind.''

''I'm not saying you don't. Only, here in Sin City it's easy to fool yourself that affection and commitment are more.''

''Affection and commitment. What am I—your new pet?'' she asked sarcastically.

''Now, you're being irrational. Once you've had a chance to calm down, we'll talk more. I bought some property outside of the city limits and I'm having plans drawn up for our new house.''

For a minute she was tempted to let him get away with changing the subject. But in the end she couldn't. Their marriage was the most important thing in the world. And she didn't want to begin it by allowing the important issues to be swept under the rug. ''We're not through talking about love. I don't want to be married to a man who doesn't love me.''

He clenched his hands into fists and she knew enough about men to know that he probably needed to get rid of his feelings with some exercise. "Angel, I care more for you than any other woman."

"I'm flattered, really I am. But I just told you I loved you and you backed away."

"Stop talking about love. It's just a word."

"If it's just a word, then why are you afraid of it?" she asked. He was a strong man. He'd made a successful life in a way few others had.

His cold graze sliced through her. "I'm not afraid of anything."

She knew she'd struck a nerve and should back away but she wasn't going to until she got to the bottom of this. Why was he so afraid of that one emotion? "We're all afraid of something. And God knows I've shown you every vulnerability I have, from my self-image to my love of romantic literature. And still you're afraid to show me yours."

"This is a crazy conversation. I'm going back to work. When you're ready to be reasonable, call me."

"Who says I'm not being reasonable?" She knew he was running. Should she let him go? Would he come back? Would she want to take him back, knowing how he felt?

"I am. Love is nothing but a word people use to justify doing things they know they'd get in trouble for otherwise."

"Is that what I'm doing?" she asked.

"Aren't you? You married me after knowing me only four days."

She'd thought they were both being swept away by their emotions. It had been the realization of her most romantic fantasy to marry him so quickly. "I married you because I love you."

"Or did you decide you love me because a whirlwind marriage is usually based on a strong physical attraction and you want to defend that decision."

She shook her head, her heart aching unbearably. "I don't have to make excuses for my behavior. Why do you?"

"Because I'm still running from my past," he said. He cursed savagely under his breath and brushed past her to go to the bar. He took a highball glass and poured himself two fingers of scotch. Fascinated, she watched as he drained the scotch in two long swallows.

"What do you want from me?" he asked.

"I'm not sure. I thought we went into this marriage wanting the same things. But today I find out you had a wager on my answer to your proposal and think love is for fools."

"Are we back to the wager again?"

"I don't think we really ever left it."

He shook his head. "Hell, I don't have the words to make this right. I never have. I'm not a smooth talker."

"You can be," she said. "When it suits you."

"Are you saying it doesn't suit me right now?"

"I don't know. I'm not sure what I'm saying."

She crossed to the pool table and leaned against it. Memories of the game they'd played swamped her and she wanted to say forget it. To say it didn't matter if he loved her. She'd be happy here.

But she'd made a promise long ago not to put herself in second place again. Not for anyone or anything. And even Deacon, with his steamy sensuality and ability to make her believe in fate, was not going to make her break that vow.

"I've got a hotel to run," he said. "We can talk about this later." With that, Deacon turned and walked out the door.

Kylie watched him leave, knowing she had no choice but to leave, too. She needed time to herself to think about the choices she'd made. And to sort out her feelings for the dark man she'd vowed to love.

Twelve

Deacon got as far as his office before he regretted walking away from Kylie. Yet he didn't have the words to make her stay. Actually he did have them, but he knew he'd never utter them. He'd heard his mom use them too many times and be wrong. He'd watched Mac's marriage fall apart because Cecelia had fallen in love with another man. He'd vowed never to let those words cross his lips. Not even Kylie was going to make him break that vow.

He had a meeting with the dealers to talk about a new incentive program. The meeting was long, and for the first time Deacon resented his role at the casino. He should have stayed upstairs with Kylie until they'd come up with a compromise that worked for both of them.

"Excuse me," he said, standing and leaving the meeting. He took the elevator to his penthouse suite and knew as soon as he entered that he'd waited too long. The place was empty. Her suitcases were gone and there was a note propped in the middle of the pool table.

He crossed the room and ripped open the envelope, then unfolded the note. Her handwriting was neat and feminine, which was no surprise.

I need some time to think about this marriage. I'll contact you when I've reached some decisions. I've always believed that love is a gift, and I hope you will use this time apart to come to terms with the gift I've given you. Like you said, sometimes fate takes time.

                                        Kylie

Deacon crumpled the note and threw it across the room. Then he left his apartment and went to the security booth to search the hotel and Vegas strip for Kylie. But he didn't see her head in the sea of people.

He called Martha and told her to call every hotel in the area to see if Kylie had checked in. Then he called her old place in Glendale, but the line had

been disconnected and his number given as a for-
warding one.

Damn. How could things that had been so perfect
a few hours earlier be so screwed up now? The door
behind him opened and he pivoted to face the person, hoping it was Martha with some news. Instead,
it was Angelo Mandetti.

"What do you need, Mandetti?" Deacon asked.
He wasn't in the mood to talk to the gaming commissioner now. A sense of desperation made the
back of his neck tingle, and he knew he had to find
Kylie quickly. Vegas wasn't kind to women on their
own. He didn't want to think of his angel out there
alone.

"I wanted to make sure Kylie was all right."

"Why wouldn't she be?" Deacon asked, trying
for a nonchalance he was far from feeling.

"She was upset after overhearing your conversation," Mandetti said.

"Hell."

"Want to talk about it, *compare?*"

Deacon bit back a curse. "Do I look like a guy
who wants to talk?"

Mandetti laughed. "No. Guys like us don't talk."

"No, we don't," Deacon said. Maybe that was
the problem. He really didn't like to talk about feelings. His mom had never said anything about it, but
he'd grown up watching men who professed to love
her, then would use her and leave her. It had left a

sour taste in his mouth. "What do we do, Mandetti?"

"If we keep acting like *babbeos*, we end up alone."

"I married her. Why isn't that enough?" Deacon asked. The question plagued him. He'd made everything picture-perfect. He'd proposed by the waterfall, gotten down on one knee. He'd flown her parents to Vegas from their vacation in Europe. He'd given her everything she could ever ask for. And he'd done it without her even having to ask.

"I'll be honest here, *compare*. Women have a different set of ideas around commitment than we do."

Deacon leaned his head back and rubbed his eyes. Mandetti didn't know the half of it. Love. She wanted love from him. Which she already had. He loved her. God, he'd never felt so much for a woman before in his entire life. He just wasn't going to say the words.

He wasn't going to let her know how deeply she'd gotten to him. How deeply she'd affected the world he'd carefully created, how it had been rocked by her presence. And now that she was gone, it seemed so…empty.

"I can't find her," Deacon said at last.

"What do you mean?"

"She's gone."

"What are you going to do?"

Deacon thought about it. He wasn't going to let

this affect him. He'd successful managed his life keeping his emotions carefully buried, and he wasn't going to change that now.

"Wait for her to return."

"What's the problem between you two? The bet?"

"Not the bet. She wants something from me I can't give her."

"What?"

Deacon wasn't sure he liked Mandetti in the role of father confessor. The man was from the gaming commission, for Pete's sake. "Never mind."

"You're giving me *agita*."

"Too bad," Deacon said. "You remind me of someone."

"Who?"

"Just a guy who used to hang around my mom. He was an enforcer and he taught me a lot about surviving."

"You've done good," Mandetti said.

"I wanted a picture-perfect marriage—that's what Kylie doesn't understand."

"What's picture-perfect?"

He wasn't going to say it out loud, because he'd sound like a sap. He should be out driving around looking for her. Except he didn't want her to know she had that much influence over him. He was going to wait for her to return, and when she did, he'd make sure she never left him again.

"Are you going after her?"

"No, I don't think so. She said she'll come back and she will."

"What if she doesn't?"

Deacon gave a wry laugh. "Then it'll prove me right."

"Listen, *compare*. You have to go after her."

"Why?"

"My job is to make sure you do."

"Your job? Since when does the gaming commission care about the personal lives of casino owners?"

"Hell, this is going to sound crazy."

"What is?"

"I'm a matchmaker sent from heaven to make sure you and Kylie get together."

"Sure you are. Listen, have you been out in the sun today?"

"*Merda*. I know I sound like a *gavone*, but it's the truth."

"Sure it is. Sit down and I'll get you some water," Deacon said, pushing the older man into one of the leather chairs. Maybe Mandetti was having a stroke. He reached for his cell phone, intending to call Martha and have her send the EMTs to the security room.

But Mandetti grabbed his arm. "This should convince you."

* * *

They flew through the air, landing in front of the mansion he planned to build for Kylie. The house was perfectly landscaped. In the circular drive was a Mercedes and his Jag.

"Where are we?"

"Five years in the future at your home."

"I must be dreaming."

"Come on, would I be in your dream?"

"Why wouldn't you? A dream is more believable than a matchmaker from heaven."

"Believe what you will. Come inside and take a look at the life you wanted."

Deacon followed Mandetti into the foyer of the house. A maid was dusting the front room, and the marble floor led to an impressive spiral staircase. In the family room he found Kylie sitting on the couch. Her hair was just like the Ralph Lauren ad in his head. Lightly highlighted and fashionably cut. She wore designer clothes and was talking to Mrs. Beauchamps from the Nevada State Historical Society.

"This is perfect," Deacon said. Clearly, Kylie was going to return and things would be good between them. Better than even he'd expected.

Mrs. Beauchamps left and he saw himself enter. Kylie didn't smile when he entered the room, and as he watched the exchange between the two of them, he realized how superficial their relationship was. He moved closer to look into her eyes, and he realized they seemed void of any emotion. He looked at himself and saw that he, too, was wearing a mask.

"How was your day?" Kylie asked. She'd stood when he entered the room. He crossed the room to kiss her, but his wife turned her face to the side and offered only her cheek.

What the hell kind of marriage did they have?

His future self let her get away with the evasion and crossed to the bar. "Good. Yours?"

"Good. Are you ready to eat?"

Deacon poured a drink and nodded.

"I'll go tell Josephine," Kylie said. She left the room. And his older self watched her go, his expression, now unmasked, one of…longing. Yes, that's what it was. Longing for something he couldn't have. Deacon saw then that his perfect life wasn't perfect. It was cold and almost lonely.

"What's this?" he asked Mandetti. This didn't fit his image of marriage, and he honestly couldn't believe this was what Kylie wanted, either.

"You wanted a marriage without love, and Kylie gave it to you. Neither of you is happy, but you project an image of the perfect couple."

"This is all wrong. I don't want that."

"Then you have to change it. Don't wait for Kylie to come back to you."

Could he do it? He knew he had to. He'd been thinking about it since the moment he'd left her alone in the penthouse suite. Some things were worth fighting for. Kylie was definitely one of them.

"You're right. I have to go to her. Talk to her." Oh, man, he was going to have to confess his feelings for her and hope that she'd meant it when she said she loved him. He didn't know if he could do it. But he had to risk it.

Hell, he'd built his life on risks. And Lady Luck hadn't abandoned him yet. He was ready to roll the dice one more time and lay everything on the line for Kylie.

Mandetti took his arm and they were back in the security booth. Deacon wondered if they'd ever really left. But then, he'd seen many things in this life that couldn't be explained, such as incredible runs of good luck that left a man a millionaire.

"You've got to help me find her," Deacon said.

Mandetti closed his eyes and a second later his pager beeped. He glanced down at the window display. "She's at a cabin in Lake Mead."

Deacon took the address from Mandetti and left. He didn't call Martha or check in with his duty manager. He just climbed into the Jag and drove out of Vegas like the devil was on his heels.

He realized that his life *was* Kylie. Any life not filled with her love wasn't worth living. He needed her by his side—not because she filled that faceless image of wife and mother in his head, but because she was the other half of his soul. She was the softness he'd never had. The dreams he'd forgotten to dream. And the love he'd always craved but never would have admitted to.

Deacon made the drive to Lake Mead in record time. She'd rented a cabin that was pretty isolated from the other buildings he saw as he pulled into the driveway and turned off his engine. He hoped he'd have the right words to win her back.

But he wasn't a romantic guy. The proposal and wedding had come from a magazine. But in real life, in this situation, he knew he had to speak from the heart. Nothing scared him more.

Own your fear or it'll own you. That one motto had kept him alive on the streets when he'd been fourteen. And he'd survived. No way was he going to let Kylie slip through his fingers. She was his wife. They'd exchanged vows.

He opened the door and wished he'd brought her a new necklace. But he had no gift. Only himself. Maybe he should sweep her into his arms and make love to her. Not give either of them a chance to talk. Talking had only gotten him in trouble the last time.

He swallowed and nervously patted his suit jacket into place. He straightened his tie and then realized he wasn't facing an arch enemy but his wife. His wife. The words echoed in his head as he approached the front door of the cabin.

He raised his hand and pounded on the door. He heard her footsteps and then the door opened. Kylie gasped when she saw him, her hand going to her throat.

"How did you find me?"

"We have a matchmaking angel helping us out."

"Deacon, are you sick?"

"Yes," he said. "I am sick."

"Come in. I'll get you some water."

"I don't need any water."

"What do you need?"

He stepped over the threshold and took her in his arms. "You."

Lowering his head, he took the kiss that he'd been craving since she'd returned to Vegas and everything had gone wrong.

Kylie willed herself not to respond to Deacon. He was here, which surprised her. She'd expected to have at least a full day before he tracked her down. She wasn't sure he'd even want to track her down.

The small cabin in Lake Mead had seemed like a good place to think. To sort out whether she wanted to be a two-time divorcée or wanted to stay in a loveless marriage. But Deacon's appearance raised questions she was afraid to answer.

She'd left because she knew how badly she wanted to stay with him. Knew in her heart that if she didn't get away and try to think this through, she'd take whatever he offered, even if it meant changing in some way. Because Deacon was the man she'd always secretly dreamed of finding, and living without him sounded cold and lonely.

She didn't know what to expect from Deacon anymore. She'd realized during the long cab ride here that she hadn't taken the time to get to know him. Her heart said she knew all she needed to know, but her mind was wary. She didn't want to be hurt again.

Yet his arms felt so right around her. For just a minute she closed her eyes and breathed deeply. But she knew she was entirely too weak where this man was concerned.

He lifted his head and looked at her. There was an intensity in his eyes she'd never seen there before. And an emotion she was scared to name. Something had changed in him in the short time they'd been apart. "I'm not leaving here without you," he said.

Her heart beat a little faster. Why had he come? She had to make sure, this time, that he wanted the same things she did. She wasn't going to jump in his arms and settle for second-best. Deacon had taught her a lot—about herself. She was worth more than he'd offered her. She deserved a husband who loved her. "I said I'd come back."

"I couldn't wait for that, angel," he said, framing her face in his hands. He rubbed his thumbs down her cheekbones. She felt incredibly fragile when he held her like this. She felt vulnerable, too, as if he could see all her weaknesses and doubts. But she also felt hope spring to life in the deepest part of her soul.

He'd come after her. No one had ever done that before.

"I can't think when you're this close," she said at last.

"Good, don't think. Just feel."

He dipped his head and nibbled at her lips. She opened her mouth and invited him in with the tip of her tongue. He thrust his into her mouth. She sensed he was trying to tell her something with that kiss, but for the life of her, she couldn't figure out what.

They were both breathing harder when he raised his head. His hands skimmed down her back and he lifted her more fully into his body. She felt his erection nudging her center. Her body softened and melted in response. She wondered if she should take him to bed and try to chain him to her with the bonds of the flesh.

No. Sexual compatibility had never been an issue between them. Only emotional agreement, and she still wasn't ready to abandon her dreams of a loving marriage.

She pulled away and walked farther into the cabin. Deacon cursed under his breath and she heard the door close with more force than necessary. She sat in a large armchair facing the windows that overlooked the lake.

Deacon paced over to her and sank onto the hassock at her feet. "Okay, I guess we may as well talk."

He sounded so in charge and in control. It frightened her to think that he didn't have any chinks in the armor he wore around his heart. That shield he used to keep everyone—even her—at bay.

"If you don't like it, you can leave," she said.

"I'm not leaving without you."

"You keep saying that but, Deacon, I'm not ready to go back to what we had."

He put his hands on her hips and pulled her forward in the chair. His legs slid along either side of hers and she felt completely surrounded by him. "I liked what we had."

"I can see why you would. But I need to be more than a prize."

He rubbed his hands over her thighs. She shivered with awareness. "Angel, you always were. It was just safer for me to think of you that way."

"Safer how?" she asked. She grabbed his wrists to stop the movement of his hands.

"Emotionally," he said. He twisted his hands in her grip and lifted both of hers to his lips. He kissed the backs of her hands and then held them together in one of his.

"Why?" she asked. Though she was trying desperately to focus on what he was saying, it was very hard.

"Dammit, I don't want to dissect this. I love you, Kylie. And you're my wife. I want us to return to Vegas and make a life together."

She could hear the blood rushing in her ears, and her heart beat so fast she thought she might have a heart attack. Of all the things she imagined him using to convince her to return, love was the one thing she hadn't dared to hope for.

"You love me?"

"Yes," he said, that intensity she'd noticed earlier shining brightly from his eyes. "Please come back home with me. My life is nothing without you."

"Oh, Deacon."

"Is that a yes?"

"Yes, it is. You know I love you, right?"

"I was betting on it."

She laughed as he scooped her up in his arms and carried her across the room to the small bedroom. He set her on her feet next to the old-fashioned bed and carefully removed her clothing, then his. And then he laid her in the center of the bed and made love to her. Later he cradled her close and rubbed her back and told her all his dreams and asked her about hers. And finally, being Deacon, he started planning how they would make them all come true. But in her heart Kylie knew as long as she had Deacon's love, everything else was in the bag.

Epilogue

"Celebrating, Mandetti?"

I was standing at a roulette table in the Golden Dream. I'd just seen Deacon and Kylie and the couple were definitely in love and together for the long haul. "Hey, babe! I'm getting good at this."

She gave me one of those haughty looks of hers. For an angel, Didi had a lot of attitude and she was tricky. "Don't get too confident."

"I'm the King of Hearts, remember. Confidence is part of the package."

"Pasquale, don't believe your own advertising."

"Why not?"

"Because you don't need a bigger head."

I threw my head back and laughed. I'd never admit it to Didi or anyone else, for that matter, but I liked this new gig. This particular job had made me feel good, because Deacon reminded me a lot of the man I could have been if I'd made different choices.

I'd never realized when I was on Earth the first time that there were choices, or that success didn't necessarily come with the title *capo*.

Madon', I sounded like a *gavone*.

"What number are you betting on, Pasquale?"

"Seven, babe, what else?"

She narrowed her eyes at me. "I'll take eleven."

The roulette wheel spun and the ball dropped on black seven for a second and then popped up to stay on red eleven. "Cheater."

"I'm an angel. I don't have to cheat."

She disappeared and I watched her go. *Madon'*, I must be getting soft from doing this job, but for a minute I actually missed her.

* * * * *

presents

DYNASTIES : THE DANFORTHS

A family of prominence…
tested by scandal, sustained by passion!

Man Beneath the Uniform
by
MAUREEN CHILD
(Silhouette Desire #1561)

He was her protector. But navy SEAL
Zachary Sheriday wanted to be more
than just a bodyguard to sexy scientist
Kimberly Danforth. Was this one seduction
Zachary was duty-bound to deny…?

Available February 2004
at your favorite retail outlet.

If you enjoyed what you just read,
then we've got an offer you can't resist!

Take 2 bestselling love stories FREE!

Plus get a FREE surprise gift!

Clip this page and mail it to Silhouette Reader Service™

IN U.S.A.
3010 Walden Ave.
P.O. Box 1867
Buffalo, N.Y. 14240-1867

IN CANADA
P.O. Box 609
Fort Erie, Ontario
L2A 5X3

YES! Please send me 2 free Silhouette Desire® novels and my free surprise gift. After receiving them, if I don't wish to receive anymore, I can return the shipping statement marked cancel. If I don't cancel, I will receive 6 brand-new novels every month, before they're available in stores! In the U.S.A., bill me at the bargain price of $3.57 plus 25¢ shipping and handling per book and applicable sales tax, if any*. In Canada, bill me at the bargain price of $4.24 plus 25¢ shipping and handling per book and applicable taxes**. That's the complete price and a savings of at least 10% off the cover prices—what a great deal! I understand that accepting the 2 free books and gift places me under no obligation ever to buy any books. I can always return a shipment and cancel at any time. Even if I never buy another book from Silhouette, the 2 free books and gift are mine to keep forever.

225 SDN DNUP
326 SDN DNUQ

Name	(PLEASE PRINT)	
Address	Apt.#	
City	State/Prov.	Zip/Postal Code

* Terms and prices subject to change without notice. Sales tax applicable in N.Y.
** Canadian residents will be charged applicable provincial taxes and GST.
  All orders subject to approval. Offer limited to one per household and not valid to
  current Silhouette Desire® subscribers.
  ® are registered trademarks of Harlequin Books S.A., used under license.

DES02   ©1998 Harlequin Enterprises Limited

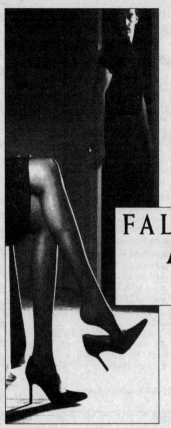
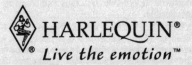

COMING NEXT MONTH

#1561 MAN BENEATH THE UNIFORM—Maureen Child
Dynasties: The Danforths
When Navy SEAL Zachary Sheriday was assigned to act as a
bodyguard to feisty Kimberly Danforth, he never considered he'd
be so drawn to his charge. Fiercely independent, and sexy, as well,
Kimberly soon had this buttoned-down military hunk completely
undone. But was this seduction one he was duty-bound to deny…?

#1562 THE MARRIAGE ULTIMATUM—Anne Marie Winston
Kristin Gordon had tried everything possible to get the attention of her
heart's desire: Dr. Derek Mahoney. But Derek's past haunted him, and
made him unwilling to act on the desire he felt for Kristin. Until one
steamy kiss set off a hunger that knew no bounds.

#1563 CHEROKEE STRANGER—Sheri WhiteFeather
He was everything a girl could want. James Dalton, rugged stable
manager, exuded sex…and danger. And for all her sweetness, local
waitress Emily Chapin had secrets of her own. One thing was
perilously clear: their burning need for each other!

#1564 BREATHLESS FOR THE BACHELOR—Cindy Gerard
Texas Cattleman's Club: The Stolen Baby
Sassy Carrie Whelan had always been a little in love with Ry Evans.
But as her big brother's best friend, Ry wasn't having it…until Carrie
decided to pursue another man. Suddenly the self-assured cowboy was
acting like a jealous lover and would do *anything* he could to make
Carrie his.

#1565 THE LONG HOT SUMMER—Rochelle Alers
The Blackstones of Virginia
Dormant desires flared the moment single dad Ryan Blackstone
laid eyes on Kelly Andrews. The sultry beauty was his son's teacher,
and Kelly's gentle manner was winning over both father and son. A
passionate affair with Kelly would be totally inappropriate…and
completely inescapable.

#1566 PLAYING BY THE BABY RULES—Michelle Celmer
Jake Carmichael considered himself a conscientious best friend. So
when Marisa Donato said she wanted a baby without the complications
of marriage, he volunteered to be the father. Their agreement was no
strings attached. But once pent-up passions ignited, those reasonable
rules were quickly thrown out the bedroom window!